Born in Clayton, New Mexico, Derek James Blan left home where his travels took him to Hawaii, California, and then further from there. Blan spent six years in Texas, where he honed his writing skills and published his first book, *Jersey Darm*, in 2016.

He also dedicates his second book, *Circadian*, to a second-oldest niece, Madeline Rose Ervin, who is a wonderful part of his life.

Derek James Blan

CIRCADIAN

AUSTIN MACAULEY PUBLISHERS™

LONDON • CAMBRIDGE • NEW YORK • SHARJAH

Ordering Information:
Quantity sales: special discounts are available on quantity purchases by corporations, associations, and others. For details, contact the publisher at the address below.

Publisher's Cataloging-in-Publication data
Blan, Derek James
Circadian

ISBN 9781645361220 (Paperback)
ISBN 9781645361237 (Hardback)
ISBN 9781645365976 (ePub e-book)

Library of Congress Control Number: 2020902966

www.austinmacauley.com/us

First Published (2020)
Austin Macauley Publishers LLC
40 Wall Street, 28th Floor
New York, NY 10005
USA

mail-usa@austinmacauley.com
+1 (646) 5125767

Blan thanks God for giving him the will and the want to create. He also thanks all those who supported him along the way.

Never take your body
Never take it for granted, never
Take it for simple romantics, never
Take it for always yours
You better hide it behind closed
Doors
Never take it for completely understood
Because it can be taken away, for good…
– Derek James Blan

Chapter 1

May 23rd, 1998 (Take the Stand)

"Look, you hid the body! You hid the body and now you want us to believe this story!" The prosecutor yells out his assumptions.

He continues to pace back and forth; he's out for blood.

He has his sleeves rolled up, sweaty and seems winded. Clearly, he has been at this for a while and is worked up over the situation. The witness sitting on the stand, getting badgered, is a young woman in her early thirties and a suspect of one of the most mysterious crimes of this century. Her name is Elizabeth Primrose.

She looks up with tears rolling down her cheek, shaken and nervous. She's getting upset because she is being badgered by this man, the prosecutor. It has gone on so long; she feels like she almost can't think straight. The amped-up prosecutor comes back in with another furry to lash out at Elizabeth.

"Where is he? What have you done?!" He leans over face-to-face, and about to continue his rant. Elizabeth goes to speak but gets cut-off by another wild out accusation.

She continues to tear up while she looks all around the room. It is a terrible feeling looking and watching time freeze while all your peers quietly judge you. Elizabeth seems to see only frowns and hatred flowing her way, from every direction.

She is interrupted by the prosecutor yelling, "Miss Primrose!"

Elizabeth feels his hot breath in her face, roaring at her. This pushes Elizabeth too far and over the line. She loses her cool and stands up and yells, "I told you the story, I told you, I don't know where the hell he went!"

The prosecutor backs up in a slight shock. He's arched back looking at Elizabeth with his guard completely up.

As if she's a terrible threat. The room comes to a halt and everyone appears quiet yet slightly shocked, staring straight at Elizabeth. Elizabeth confused, stands up on the stand with her wild expression, and tears of confusion pouring out of her.

***

A splash of water brings Elizabeth out of her "day-dream." Back to her reality in the courthouse bathroom. The water splashes out of Elizabeth's hands and onto her new dress. She is overthinking everything and she knows it.

She seems to be deliberately making herself more terrified and confused about what is actually going to happen in that courtroom today. She leans up against the sink and wipes off the water stain from her dress. She is dressed beautifully. She's trying to look good and for being a certified nurse; she believes in being presentable.

She takes a deep breath. She continues to lean up against the bathroom sink. She's not wanting to, but she's ready to go into the courtroom. She's not sure what to think; she doesn't even know how all of this is going to go down.

She looks in the mirror and a flashback of that awful night comes back into her imagination. It's as if she's standing right there at that moment, once again. It's dark and a ghastly scream comes from an even darker corner. The lights in Elizabeth's imagination flicker followed with another scream.

She remembers that night ever so clearly. She grasped the gun tight, blood covering the walls and the floor. Elizabeth takes a deep breath and gets closer to the dark corner of her imagination…then a *blast* of unavoidable interruption. The bathroom door gets a knock.

A man's voice pulls Elizabeth back to her terrifying reality. "Are you okay in there? Elizabeth?"

Another knock, then Elizabeth's defendant waves his arm inside the door.

He follows it up with, "Elizabeth, they're ready for us." He yells it from outside of the woman's restroom. Elizabeth takes a deep breath and gets a kick out of her defendant as she tries to smile. He only waves his arm in the door, afraid to go in.

She clears her somewhat bruised face and dries her hands off. She replies, "You can come in. It's only me in here."

"Are you sure?"

"Yes."

"No, it's okay. I'll wait out here…well okay then." Wilson slowly pulls open the door with his frail arm. He has grey hair, a wrinkled-face, old, and confident. Wilson stands tall wearing a nice suit, ready for court.

"Shall we?"

***

The large courtroom doors swing open. The entire room comes to a halt. They all simultaneously turn to see one of the last survivors from that horrific night. Elizabeth Primrose stands under the arched, doorframe, the entrance to the courtroom.

She feels life gets stolen from her. Her breath stops and her blood drops. Elizabeth stands in the doorway clearly frail from the event. But as an esteemed nurse, she stands her ground with her head up.

Elizabeth attempts to gain control of all her emotions. She is still nervous over this entire situation, and her imagination still plays tricks on her. It has already given her the worst outlook on all of this. Elizabeth is a little tense squeezes her fist tight.

The courtroom still watches her every move, right from the moment she opened the doors. Behind Elizabeth is Wilson. He towers over her in the shadows. The old, skinny man drained of this situation. He has heard this story thoroughly with all the details, all the twists, and turns.

Wilson in a weird, state of mind simply from knowing exactly why Elizabeth is entering the courtroom on this day. He feels for the young woman, and the trauma she had to endure. In his heart, he truly doesn't know how this one is going to turn out, considering the evidence and the story. Wilson's frail hand sets on Elizabeth's shoulder providing a small level of support.

He then gives Elizabeth a tiny push. She moves forward with a slight feel of encouragement. She enters the courtroom with the help and support of Wilson and for once she feels like she has some sort of back up. With a deep breath, Elizabeth makes her way into the center of the courtroom, ready for what's to come.

The crowd turns back around simultaneously, breaking the silence. Elizabeth fights her emotions walking in, but the weight gets heavier when she sees her mother. Elizabeth's mother is overwhelmed and sits in tears. Elizabeth smiles and tries to give the loving women some sort of hope.

Hope that everything will be fine. While Elizabeth walks to her right she sees a nurse, a handler. She sits with a confused weeping Mr. Garner. Seeing him drops Elizabeth's stomach, it's the one parent of Bruce Garner. The victim, well…the real reason why everyone is here and in tears.

The final steps lie in front of her, straight up to the judge's stand in the front of the courtroom. Elizabeth gets hit with a breath of fresh air finally a smile. This one smile gets her attention, and it is quickly followed by another. It's her two good friends attempting to show her support.

Tamara and Jordan. The courtroom is calm and the trial has already started. The prosecutor already makes his opening statements. He is the first person to get Elizabeth's full attention.

She locks eyes on him. He doesn't appear as mean and cruel as in her daydream, but he clearly didn't get where he is by being nice. The prosecutor is clean-cut and handsome. He stands presentably addressing the jury.

He looks them over and finishes his opening statement, "And it is up to you! Ladies and Gentleman…to know! And to see the truth. The truth behind the evidence that is presented here today. I ask for one thing, and for one thing alone. That is for you all to be clear on this understanding of what we are dealing with. Thank you for your time."

He closes with a calm, welcoming voice. The prosecutor turns away from the jury to take his seat. He makes eye contact with Elizabeth. She walks down to her seat that is right next to him.

He gives her a stern look and walks to his chair. Elizabeth making her way to the front of the courtroom; swallows hard. She feels once the eye contact with him was made that with her every step, her heart beats faster. Wilson keeps slightly pushing her down the aisle.

Elizabeth looks out at the number of faces and no smiles, no sense of hope, or reasoning on why this happened. Elizabeth walks down to her seat. While she sits, she attempts to smile at the judge, but he just grumbles a little and slouches in his seat. He continues to look over a few notes.

Elizabeth takes her seat with her back up, Wilson. Elizabeth looks up to Wilson as he stays standing and quickly gets ready to give his opening statement. Elizabeth looks past Wilson to the prosecutor sitting across the way, and then her eyes look over to the jury. Wilson takes a deep breath and looks down at Elizabeth and smiles.

He tries to make her feel a tad bit more comfortable. He walks out to the floor and with a stern voice addresses the jury, "Thank you, everyone, for giving me this opportunity to give my opening. Followed with my outlook on exactly why we are here today."

He turns and nods to the judge. Then turns to the jury with a smile and gestures over to Elizabeth. With a calm voice continues, "The witness here, Miss. Primrose, is no suspect. Not a suspect that is why, she wears all civilian clothing. That is also why we walk together so casually. She is not a suspect, but a witness. Miss Elizabeth Primrose."

Wilson's arm stretched out pointing toward Elizabeth. Wilson paces a little then continues. "She is here to help you. To help all of us understand what happened in that terrible place, on that terrible evening. Only two nights ago. She is here to help us, and all of us need to judge from her experience."

He looks back and with complete sincerity, he looks into the eyes of the jury. Then around to the judge. He continues, "Now I've heard this story quite a few times and I'm with warning to tell you that it's not for the faint of heart. There are reasons there are only the two witnesses left alive and what Miss Primrose had to endure."

Wilson puts his hand over his mouth. He has his breath taken away by the thought. He attempts to continue, "What this woman had to endure, you will only agree that this was all rare and terrible. But you will also agree that the one at fault, if anyone, is still at large. Now let me continue with confidence, that this jury. That this arrangement of peers will come to a conclusion on who to hold responsible and accountable for this incident. Thank you all once again."

***

Elizabeth's nails grip the armrest in the hot seat. Elizabeth takes the stand and looks out over her peers. She's able to keep her composer. She looks over to the judge on her right.

The prosecutor gets up and struts out and around his table. He stops and goes through his notes that already lay spread out on the table. He looks them over and seems to takes a few seconds for himself. He reaches over, pulls out his glasses, and at the same time smiles and flirts with the jury.

He casually grabs a piece of paper studies it and continues to take his time. The impatient judge grumbles under his breath, which working together for so long, the prosecutor knows that means, move it. Elizabeth loses her breath and the memories are fading, but she knows they will never truly leave her mind. She shakes it off attempting to be patient.

She's sure this is a technique. Maybe to make the person on the stand lose their train of thought by a combination of anxiety and unnecessary patience. The prosecutor makes his way to the stand, stops mid-stride, and makes eye contact with Elizabeth. He puts out his hand smiles, and proceeds, "Well, let us start with your opinion, your statement miss Primrose. Primrose, is it?"

"Yes, Elizabeth Primrose." Elizabeth was hoping they would just let her talk, but the prosecutor seems to take all control.

The prosecutor is a prick, but still not as bad as Elizabeth had imagined. He walks back and forth looking at Elizabeth, "Miss. Primrose? Why don't we start with your simple outlook on the situation we are in."

She shakes off the trauma of actually sitting in this seat, especially for this situation, for this reason. She knows it has to start here, and the world is about to find out the horrible truth about Bruce Garner. The truth about Bruce, and about life itself, as humans perceive it. Elizabeth fights back, but the tears already begin, and so does she.

"There is a myth. A myth that when a man sleeps, he is out of the body, but eventually returns. Well, that's only half true. You are always with your body even as it rests. But it's the other half of you. The other half is a former entity that is in the body, and once you sleep that's what leaves, but doesn't come back. Because it's replaced."

The prosecutor trying his best to understand her gibberish, but is confused. The judge and her defense attorney Wilson make eye contact, but the judge lets her continue. "The entity that leaves is only here for that day. Here to help shape and mold you. Forcing situations, obligations…and I believe…"

The prosecutor hearing her loud and clear, but does what he does best and cuts off her rant. "I'm so sorry to have to stop you in the middle of the first lines of your outlook. But what does any of this have to do with Mr. Garner?"

Elizabeth makes eye contact and another tear rolls down her cheek, but you can tell the prosecutor has seen it all before.

He's clearly not phased. Elizabeth feels his lack of emotions and wipes her tear, and then turns her attention to the jury. "I'm sorry if I'm being too far out there. I'm only trying to make you understand where I'm going with this. As a nurse, I've seen a lot, but this…"

Elizabeth adjusts herself and tries to get back on her game with another deep breath. "The human body is washed clean every night when you sleep, and when you wake, it's a completely different entity forming your body. Alongside with you. A force that gives the body a different experience for a short period of time and you change every day. You never are the same again. You will always be you, but this force is how we grow."

The prosecutor once again interrupts Elizabeth and her rant, "Wow, wow! Let's slow down. Wow, you know what? Let's start at the beginning of all this. When did you first meet Bruce Garner?"

Elizabeth for once gets a tiny smile on her face. She smiles over her memories of Bruce. Elizabeth gets dreamy-eyed and replies, "Well, Bruce jogged. It was the…" Elizabeth pauses not from memory loss, but the complete opposite.

She pauses from remembering too much at once. She continues on, "He was always jogging."

Chapter 2
May 4th, 1998 (Bruce Garner)

A used running shoe gets thrown casually on the carpet. Bruce Garner flops himself down on the couch and then drops the second shoe in front of him. Bruce reaches down and grabs the first shoe, slides it on over his right foot. He leans over and ties his shoe then sits up and leans back, trying to get the motivation to do this run.

He looks around at his lavish apartment while his music plays loud. It plays loud with aggression to give him energy or any spark of reason that's needed for this run. Bruce wears jogging shorts and a sweatshirt. He is a handsome man. He is healthy, fit, and clearly determined.

He leans back and throws his foot on the glass table that sits in front of him to tie his second shoe. He looks down at his worn-out running shoes draped across his feet. The lack of whiteness on his shoes and shoelaces proves he jogs every day, if not more.

He sees how worn his running shoes are, and almost hates even tying the dirty things, for being a clean freak.

Bruce finishes beating around the bush. He is just putting off this run. He knows once the run is started it goes a lot smoother. It's getting started that's the hard part.

He looks like he's trying to do life right, as he jumps off the couch. He gets to his feet and stretches before his run. He takes the breathing and timing very seriously but is quickly distracted by Oscar. His cat, meowing out for attention.

Oscar runs up to Bruce's feet, meows, and rubs on him. Bruce smiles and with a sly comment, "You have to wait till I start stretching to beg for food?" Bruce pats Oscar on the head. They head to the kitchen, to feed Oscar.

Bruce throws food in the bowl then watches Oscar attack the food like he's starving. Bruce watches him then looks at his watch, distracted by his daily routines. He loves his cat, but his schedule now has his complete attention. Bruce sets the timer on his watch for his morning run.

He gives Oscar an extra pat on the head and rushes to the front door. He stops and turns around. He grabs his shades off the side table. He pauses for a moment longer then sees his key with a small red sleeve covering it as it sits on the side table.

He grabs the key and throws it in the air, catches it and puts it in his pocket. Then turns and walks out the door.

***

Bruce jogs through a park. It's a calm inviting place on a beautiful day. Everything is green and bright. He is keeping a steady pace while he looks around at the world.

The vibe of this situation, this run is strong. Bruce feels it, a soul-cleansing jog feels wonderful. Bruce controls his breathing and pays full attention to his path that he has decided to take. He takes another leaping step up and over a break in the sidewalk and onto a paved path into the trees.

A path that was made especially for joggers. Bruce's breath is steady as he runs without slowing his pace one bit. Bruce takes turns with ease. It's clear, it's not his first time to run through this park.

He loves it. He picks up speed into a slight sprint through the curves. The body has laws, and one is; you will slowly burn out with a sprint. Bruce is no different. He lets up and slows back to his normal jogging pace.

He has to catch his breath. He looks around at all the nature surrounding him. It's a big part of why he loves running in this park. It's beautiful.

Bruce feels that he woke up on the wrong side of the bed this morning. Bruce feels slightly different, too much on his mind. He feels tired, and hoping, the sprint; the jog will help wake him up. Help him clear his mind.

Bruce passes other runners with slight nods. Nods of understanding to the pain of the run, and the joy of it. A runner jogs off to the side giving Bruce room to run by. Bruce nods in understanding.

It's almost a blur like they know each other, but only from the passing wave that has happened a million times. Bruce feels a little winded, he keeps getting distracted by his shoelace. It flips up and down into the air brushing up against his leg. He keeps getting pulled back into this existence, back into a jogging-body.

He hates to do it, but he needs to stop. Bruce knows there is a wooden bench around the corner. He keeps his pace and makes it around the corner and no doubt the bench sits, untouched. Bruce stops, lets the blood flow to his legs and then shakes off the strain.

He paces back and forth tries to catch his breath. He throws his foot upon the bench. He intends on fixing the constant distraction from the run, tying his shoe. He doesn't want to calm his body too much and needs to pick up the pace.

There's a rustle coming out from the bushes. It gets Bruce's attention immediately. He looks around and sees no one, not another runner, nothing. Bruce pauses then looks deeper into the brush and down the path.

A calm voice interrupts him from behind, "Sir? Is this yours?" Bruce is interrupted by a homeless man standing right behind him.

Bruce looks down at the man from the difference in posture and character. The homeless man looks up to Bruce with sad eyes, trying his hardest to make his madness look friendly. The homeless man holding a spare key with a red cover over the top of it. He holds it high up to Bruce.

It's Bruce's key and it's clear to the homeless man when Bruce frantically pats himself down. Bruce is in shock over the realization he almost lost his house key. The homeless man smiles and hands it over. Bruce smiles gratefully for his generosity.

Bruce takes the key and simply replies, "Thank you." Bruce smiles and puts his key in a new pocket, then turns to walk away, but quickly feels compelled to give the man something in return. Coincidentally, Bruce has a simple fold. A few one dollars wrapped around a five-dollar bill.

Bruce turns and stops the man from walking away and forcing the fold into his hand. Bruce feels good, but the man turns to him almost confused holding the money out. Bruce looks the man over and feels like he needs to at least explain himself.

"That's another thank you. I don't know if you need it, but thank you. It's just, I really need this key."

***

"Miss Primrose? I'm not sure what this has to do with the reason why we are here." The prosecutor interrupts her story. He stands off to the side of his table.

He has both arms tight across his chest. He gets a little snicker and then looks down at Wilson sitting at his table. He stands upright and asks out loud, "Is she serious right now? Miss Primrose, we are here to learn about that night. I don't see how any of this has to do with any of it."

Elizabeth takes a breath, "I'm simply trying to explain to everyone what kind of character Bruce was…is."

The prosecutor takes over, "I see, so what type of man was he Miss Primrose?"

Elizabeth looks over everyone and continues, "He cared a lot about people. I'm only pointing this out because I feel his name shouldn't be cursed or hated. He was once a great man."

The prosecutor stands and just stares and goes to ask another question. "It's good to know who we are talking about, you're right. But how can a simple story of generosity make us look away from what he is?"

Elizabeth sits upright and adjusts, "I just want everyone to know he's a human."

Bruce picks up his pace and never looks back, but he is extremely thankful for that man finding his house key. Then in a paranoid thought. He checks himself over for his other properties. They're all in place.

Bruce stays on pace and takes another turn, once again almost without even thinking or hesitating. Bruce concentrates on his breathing; he knows it's about time for him to get back to his place. He feels the body adjust and tries to get comfortable. Then out of paranoia he checks himself once again for his house key, and to make sure he has all of his possessions. And just like that Bruce is back to thinking of the homeless man.

Bruce remembers his old self to be different; not being nice to anyone, much less a homeless man. Bruce tries to understand what he was thinking back in those days, so different. He was like a completely different person. He hated and he was so angry.

To this day, Bruce is still confused about why he would wake up like that, like a completely different person. Most people say that when you begin to act like you're losing control to take a nap, like a cleansing.
The thought in itself actually makes Bruce a little tired, but he shakes it off.

Bruce comes over a hill. He sees the end of the path, out of the trees and back into the park. Bruce knows now that his apartment is right around the corner. Three minutes of jogging time.

Bruce doesn't stop until he's up to the third floor of his complex building. He comes up to room C3. Bruce is out of breath from the run. He searches himself over for the key.

He pulls it out of his pocket.

Bruce goes to use his key, but stops…the door is unlocked. In most situations, this would be a clear sign for alarm, but Bruce wears a slight grin and then barges into his apartment. Bruce barges in out of breath and covered in sweat he comes in to see a beautiful woman. She's sitting on his couch, watching his television, and holding Oscar.

Bruce relieved walks up and gives Elizabeth Primrose a kiss on the head. She smiles up at him, after kissing her Bruce falls over the arm of the couch practically on top of her.

Elizabeth cries out. "Gross honey! You're all sweaty."

Bruce smiles big just happy to be around her, "I missed you much! Oh hell, I left the door open."

Elizabeth pushes him off of her while he jumps up. Bruce struts over and closes the door.

He comes running back to Elizabeth. She laughs out loud, smiles then she leans in and kisses him.

She smiles and replies, "I missed you too. Now go shower."

Bruce still filling a little pumped after his run, walks past the couch into the hallway and into the back room. He takes his shirt off. Elizabeth looks back over the couch, watching him. A smile spread across her face.

Bruce gets to the doorway and looks back to Elizabeth. He gestures for her to follow.

***

Elizabeth sits on the stand, back in the courtroom trying her best to hold her composer. She seems to be out of breath while she's telling her story. She's trying to answer the questions that are being looked for. The prosecutor stands staring blankly at Elizabeth.

Elizabeth just keeps seeing Bruce in her imagination, and her eyes water. It seems a while before the prosecutor says anything. The judge adjusts himself in his seat next to Elizabeth, also waiting for the process to continue.

The prosecutor chuckles slightly, then says, "So, you already knew Bruce? You knew Bruce before the day he went into your hospital?"

Elizabeth feels a little battered, but she also never had to take the stand before today. Elizabeth not holding back says, "Yes. I met him a few months before that day."

"How did you two meet? If you don't mind me asking?"

Elizabeth looks over to the prosecutor and with a stern voice,

"Jogging."

The prosecutor paces back and forth then with a slight assertiveness asks, "Did you have an intimate relationship with Bruce, Mr. Garner?"

The judge interrupts the process with sternness to reach the truth. "What does that, have to do with any of this?"

The prosecutor with slight defensiveness says, "I'm just trying to get to the bottom of their relationship." Elizabeth has a single tear roll down her cheek, feels insulted.

But she is just as confused as all of these people sitting before her. She feels the need to be completely open to everyone. She interrupts the argument that was most likely going to continue, "Yes! Yes, I did."

The prosecutor stops with a slight grin. He looks to the judge and gestures. "Shall I continue?"

He moves closer toward Elizabeth, "So you would have known him pretty well, right?"

With a straight face covered with honesty, Elizabeth answers, "Somewhat. We started dating and we were together for maybe two and a half months before…everything."

The prosecutor walks away with haste yelling over the room. "So, you say, two and a half months? So that's a good amount of time to get to know someone. From my records, it shows you two were inseparable right off the bat. I mean already having a key. Not to mention dinner receipts, movie tickets. A receipt for new jogging shoes."

The prosecutor drops the paper he was looking at. "Look I don't want to point out the obvious, but you guys were together so what happened that night? I honestly want to know, and I'm positive your peers want to know where he is. Why he's missing?"

Elizabeth looks over the blank stares of her peers that are entertained at her struggle. A newfound fear of what the human is capable of. She looks at the prosecutor with another tear rolling out of her eyes.

She continues, "I did know him well. We were getting very close, very fast, until that night. The night it all changed. The night my reality opened a new door. A door that I will never get closed again."

Chapter 3
May 5th, 1998 (Wrong Street)

The dim lighting of the dinner surface is peaceful at a very nice exclusive restaurant. It's set to a calm tone for all who dine. A sincere high-class tone. The tables are decorated and covered in a silky white tablecloth.

Bruce has the white tablecloth in his hand, and he pretends to blow his nose into it. Bruce is suited up and dressed to impress. Elizabeth gets a kick at him acting like a goof. She gets a laugh and then attempts to kick him under the table.

She actually lands one on his shin. She kicks him and then quietly says, "Stop, or I will make a scene." Bruce sits up straight and acts more mature. He reaches over and grabs Elizabeth's hand. She feels comfortable with Bruce, he makes her laugh. They make eye contact and they end up holding it for a while longer this time around. Bruce breaks the tension and looks at his watch. Shakes his head in eagerness.

"Where is this food? I was hoping to get to eat and spend a little more time with you before you have to go back to work."

Elizabeth squeezes his hand and replies, "We have plenty of time, we can sit here and enjoy our food." Bruce smiles at her.

"You're right, you know I just really like your company." Bruce squeezes back returning the happiness. Their grasp is quickly broken by a steaming-hot plate. It comes over the two of them from their waiter's grasp.

They release each other and sit back with smiles. Bruce smiles and says, "I guess I spoke too soon." They both cover themselves with a napkin and begin to eat their dishes. Elizabeth is trying to be proper and take her time, enjoy her food, but she's hungry.

Bruce is reacting to his meal in the exact same manner. It is clear, no words are being spoken for their entree. The waiter makes his rounds once again and notices his table 33 is actually communicating and laughing again. They must be almost finished with their plates.

He makes his way over to them, very casually. He goes to grab Bruce's plate, it's spotless. The waiter simply utters the word, "Dessert?"

***

Bruce splashes his face with a timed water faucet. He waves his hand under the sink once again trying to force some sort of action. The bathroom attendant is a short butler. He doesn't say much to Bruce to apply any form of support.

Click, the water stops again. Bruce rubs his hand over his face and then again proceeds to wave his hand under the facet. The attendant rolls his eyes casually and then reaches over to a dry towel and holds it out. *Click*, the water starts to run once more, and Bruce finally gets enough water to splash his face clean.

Bruce looks over and sees the bathroom attendant patiently holding the towel out for him. Bruce takes the towel and pats himself dry, turning away and looking back to the mirror. He casually pulls a tiny box from his pocket, looks it over. It's a gift.

The bathroom attendant smiles and once again rolls his eyes. Bruce puts the box back in his pocket. He then reaches in another pocket and pulls out a few dollars to tip the attendant. Bruce looks in the mirror one last time.

This time Bruce gives himself the look of courage, to give his gift to Elizabeth. He smiles in the mirror then at the attendant and makes his way out of the men's bathroom. He has a noticeably different strut, as he walks through the restaurant back to their table. He comes around the back of Elizabeth and places his hand on her shoulder.

He comes around and sits back down in his seat. He smiles at Elizabeth and her plate is already gone. Bruce reaches across the table and grabs Elizabeth's hand and slightly squeezes. He stares at her.

"You look very beautiful tonight. What do you feel like doing after this?" Elizabeth about to answer, but their grasp is broken once again by the waiter. He shows up with their beautiful dessert. Bruce pulls back, and the waiter places the slice of dessert in front of the two of them. Elizabeth smiles, and that in return makes Bruce smile even larger. Once again, they both get their napkins and cover their lap. Bruce grabs his fork and waits for her to take the first bite.

He then takes a nice fork full and loves it. Elizabeth grabs a fork and scoops it on a separate plate. Bruce takes a second bite. He chews and wipes his mouth and then waves his hand.

"I'm finished. That's just too much for me." He looks at the cake one last time and quickly grabs up his fork again.

"You know, today has actually been very strange for me. It has been extremely positive. I have been somewhat of a cluts though, but I guess we all have our ups and downs. You know our different days."

Bruce finishes and takes another bite. Apparently, he forgot he already had enough. Elizabeth nods in agreement over what Bruce is saying, but in reality, his comments got her selfishly thinking about her own day. She nibbles and thinks how she doesn't really feel like she lived her life to the fullest today. Or any other day for that matter.

She goes to speak and give any form of a reply but gets cut-off. Her phone goes off in her lap. Bruce stops talking altogether as Elizabeth's phone gets louder. He takes another small bite and awkwardly smiles. Elizabeth takes another nibble and casually looks at her phone.

She knows it's work calling for her. She's right. The message blares out bright on the screen. 'We need you here NOW!'

Her shoulders slump and once Bruce sees this, he already knows what's about to happen. He's getting to know her routine better and better. He realizes she's leaving and he isn't going to get any form of response about anything. He also realized he isn't going to get an, "anything after."

The awkward frown/smile coming from the two of them is a hard thing to ignore. A couple of simple apology jesters come from them. Elizabeth slides her chair out, not happy to see Bruce sad.

"I've got to go…they need me. I got dinner tonight, but you owe me one. I'll call you in a bit." She walks around and throws some money on the table, bends down and gives him a kiss on the cheek.

He looks up at her trying to be understanding. "Work is work you know. Go get it done, but come by in the morning if you want to. I'm going home now…well after dessert."

He finishes with a smile. Elizabeth bends down and kisses him and then exits the restaurant, quickly to the panic of her career. Bruce looks across the table and puts another fork full in his mouth. He smiles playing cool while he grasps the present in his pocket. The one he doesn't get to give.

***

A plate glass window sits clean and clear. You can see through it, and see it's a dark night outside. This plate-glass window sits along with a dozen others on this vacant garage wall. The clean window gets instantly distorted and smashed!

A wooden baseball bat crashes through the window. Then for the hell of it, the culprit attached tightly at the handle smashes another one and another one. The young burglar wears all black in baggy clothes with his face shaded. He lets himself into the house.

He walks around the vacant house's garage, nothing inside. The house is up for sale and it's empty. The young man already knew that. He turns on the light switch with aggression.

He only knew he wanted to be in this house. He wasn't really sure what to do when he got inside. He paces back and forth totally hostile and hungry for something. He grips the bat tighter at the handle and then breaks more windows in aggression.

Demolishing the windows and in return putting nicks and embedding glass throughout the wooden bat. The bat smashes a piece of glass that had fallen to the ground. He swings down, then another piece shatters on the garage concrete floor. The bat smashes down, the garage floor is covered in shattered glass.

His tight grasp releases the bat's handle. The bat falls to the broken glass with a crunch. He looks at the house's one doorway to the inside. He goes into terrible thoughts.

He places his foot on the bat and rolls it around in the glass. He reaches into his back pocket and pulls out some black leather hand gloves. The crunch of the glass echoes throughout the empty garage. He continues to crunch the glass under the bat as he rolls it around.

The garage looks smashed up. With his face shaded; he lights up a smoke and throws his lighter back in his back pocket. He leans down and grabs the glass-covered bat from the garage floor. He takes a long drag and looks at his wooden friend.

He looks up to the light bulb hanging over his head and takes another drag. He swings the bat uncontrollably and crashes the lights out.

Bruce walks up to his apartment, in a complete daydream. He steps up on the curb to the sidewalk. Bruce knows his doorway is up a few feet so he is already reaching for his house keys. They're not in his pocket. "Not again."

He stops altogether frantically searching himself over. He pulls out the gift he was going to give to Elizabeth, smiles. He puts it back in his pocket. He stops wearing a troubled look on his face, as it changes to a pure expression of concern.

An older frail man stands at his doorway. It's Bruce's father. Bruce walks up to him expressing a completely concerned voice, "Dad?" Bruce picks up the pace to get to him.

His dad stares off. "Dad, are you okay? What are you doing here?" Bruce doesn't know why he's here on the street.

He's supposed to be being watched at the New County nursing home. Bruce concerned grabs his dad's arm and sits him down on the doorstep. Bruce smiles at him, while his dad rambles off, "I'm fine! I'm fine! I just couldn't be around those dilly whackers anymore!"

Bruce's dad mumbles off in a dramatic pissed off state. Bruce smiles, "What? Those dilly what?"

"Oh, I don't know. Those damn people at the home. I needed a smoke! So...I walked over." His dad calms and smiles an old man smile at him, at his son.

Bruce hugs him. "It's good to see you." Bruce shuffles through his pockets again looking for his key. He throws his head back in disappointment.

He remembers leaving the keys on the television and then walking out of his apartment earlier today. He puts his head up against the door in despair. His dad pulls a smoke from his jacket pocket and mumbles off. "Those damn dilly whackers…they stole my matches!"

"No one stole anything from you, Dad." Bruce looks down at his dad searching frantically over himself for his matches. Bruce remembers and kneels down to his dad. "Dad, do you have my house key? I think I remember giving you a copy a few months ago."

"Not me…"

"Dad?"

"If I had it, I would have been inside already." His dad says this in a very arrogant voice.

Bruce unconvinced grabs up his dad. "I don't think so. You always keep everything especially keys."

Bruce stands him back up again and grabs his pocket chain off his jeans. Sure enough, a keyring is attached at the end. Bruce brings it out of his pocket, and the number of keys on the ring almost makes Bruce faint. Bruce and his dad look down in shock.

"Really? Why do you have all these?"

His dad shrugs and replies, "Not sure." Bruce takes in a deep breath. He unlatches the keys and goes for his door's lock.

***

Bruce helps his father up the last flight of stairs. This climb has already been a nightmare. That was after Bruce fought with the million and one keys to get in. He went through each one before luckily, he found the one to his place.

Bruce and his father stumble in. Bruce sets his father down on the sofa. His dad still searches through his pockets for his matches, with a smoke between his lips. Bruce shakes his head at his father

"We have to get you back to the nursing home." His dad finally finds an old piece of timber and strikes the match.

Bruce's dad laughs, "It's the only one I've hidden. They never found it."

Bruce yells at him while he walks to the back. "No one's stealing from you, Dad." Bruce hears his dad strike the match then suck in deep. Bruce comes from the back to see his dad smoking.

"No. No, let me have it." Bruce swings at his dad's smoke. His father puts up his finger to his son, with a stern father look.

He takes a long drag and then hands it over to Bruce. Bruce walks over to the sink and runs it under the water. Bruce walks back toward his dad wipes his hands off. "Thank you."

Bruce sees the keys sitting on top of the television. He walks over and goes to grab the keys, but knocks them down to the floor. Bruce instantly goes to grab them but kicks them under the couch where his dad sits. Bruce bends down and looks under the couch.

Oscar is there and in the way. Bruce smiles and in a baby voice, "Hey! Baby boo." Then waves Oscar off and grabs the keys.

He comes up winded. His dad just stares blankly at him. "You alright there, Sally?" Bruce gets up, winded.

"We need to get you back. I'm going to change and then we will go."

"Or I can stay here. You know to look over things. Play with the… what the hell's his name… cat." The old man pulls out another smoke and puts it between his lips, and again begins to look over his pockets for his matches.

"Damn people! I know they took my matches."

Bruce looks at his father and smiles, "I wish, Dad, but you know you need full-time supervision. Which amazes me the home still hasn't called." Bruce goes off to change. His dad continues to look over himself for his matches.

***

Bruce dressed for a run, helping his dad up the handicapped ramp. They're back at the nursing home down the street. They are finally here, after two different bus stops. Riding with a dozen or so out of this world characters.

Bruce walks with his dad inside the building through a set of sliding open doors. He walks in and waves to a group of nurses in the corner. One of the nurses gets a wheelchair and then heads their way. Bruce waves and then a tight, little pinch comes from his butt.

He turns around to see a feisty little old lady, with a firm grasp on his butt. She sees him turn around and look at her and she winks and gives a thumbs up. A nurse walks up with a wheelchair. Bruce's dad takes his seat and continues searching through his pockets.

"Finally, here? Good! Because I need to ask you dilly whackers a question! Which one of you stole my matches?"

Bruce bends down to his dad, but not too quick. He looks to see where the little old lady is. He bends down to his dad and says, "Dad, you shouldn't be smoking these anyway." Bruce goes to grab the smoke, but the nurse stops him.

"We prefer just to let him keep the smokes it keeps him calm."

The nurse playfully (mouths) "but we steal his matches."

Bruce gets a wide-eyed expression, and the nurse continues, "Thank you for finding him. They just noticed he was missing a few minutes ago."

"Well he got all the way to the third street, and he also got all the way back so. Please be more alert. It's my dad."

Bruce leans down again, "Well, I'm off pop. Don't give these nurses too hard of a time and please stay here where they can see you."

Bruce hugs his dad and smiles at the nurse. His dad mumbles up, "I will, once they give me back my timber." Bruce smiles, turns, and leaves the nursing home. Walking down the ramp; he looks off down the street.

Streetlights shine bright, and Bruce is ready for another jog. He looks at his watch, and it reads, 9:48 p.m. He shrugs it off. He has a lot to think about.

He's not sure how to handle everything and just to add, now hoping his dad will be alright in this place.

Bruce takes a jumping start into a jogging sprint. He jogs up to a fork in the road. He gets on the curb and looks to the right, then to the left. He does a few shoulder shrugs, and then a few second counts on toe touches.

He jumps up high in the air, repeatedly and mumbles to himself. "Which… way… do I…want…to go?" He is completely stretched out, loosened up, and ready for his jog. Bruce is contemplating on which route to take.

The park side is a scenic route. Which is right or the curb bridge route which is left. He enjoys both, but Bruce needs some time in his head. A little time to daydream and he knows he won't get that from the curb jog, which is left. Bruce doesn't actually seem to care which route, left or right.

He almost wishes he could run them both. He wants a little awareness, and maybe a little on your toes running. The kind the curb jog provides, so maybe, left. Bruce has a plan and turns right, and takes the scenery park route.

He runs off down a trail. He thinks to himself, wondering if there is a shortcut from one trail to the next. He has a plan that maybe he can have both kinds of jogs. He's never done it before, but hey 'there's a first time for everything.'

Bruce runs through the dark woods. He knows this path with his eyes closed, it's a calming run. It's so quiet. It's amazing how everything is already asleep out in the woods.

No birds, no movement, and no noise. Bruce thinks deeply. He thinks of his path; concentrating on his breathing. In deep thought, Bruce remembers that there is a far-off path that cuts behind the houses on Amber Street.

If he remembers correctly, he can cut through there and have the pleasure of both paths, both types of jogs.

Bruce runs for a little while longer. He's actually getting winded; he knows the turn off to Amber Street is just a little ways up. He's glad because taking Amber Street is three times faster and he wants to get home already. He almost feels like this jog was a bad idea.

He shakes away the negative thoughts and keeps pushing. He comes over a hilltop and sees Amber Street off to the far left.

The moon cuts through, shining down just right. Bruce can clearly see the path now at the bottom of the hill.

It cuts behind a few houses. It then turns into an alley that intersects with Amber Street. Then he can curb jog from Amber Street straight home. Bruce runs down from the hilltop down to the small cut-away little path.

The rough path slows him down, but then he takes an abrupt left into a dark alleyway. He slows his jog even more, not sure what's back here. It's hard to see. Bruce sees traffic in the distance happy to see Amber Street laying up ahead.

He walks calmly, but on edge for some off reason. His senses are going crazy. This alley only has tall fences and it's hard for him to see anything. He slows his breathing and cautiously walks through hoping not to trip or fall.

Then crash a window shatters! It happens actually really close to where Bruce is walking. He feels a panic come over him. He doesn't know if this is common around here or what.

He picks up pace about to jog, but then another crash. This time it was on his immediate right. He stops and gets on guard. He sees a broken window with the glass still swinging…This just happened.

Bruce looks and then turns to pick up the pace to get out of there. He turns to run, but stops and freezes in fear. He stares at a tall, cloaked man, with black gloves holding a glass-covered bat. Without saying a word, he leans on the bat and pulls a lighter from his back pocket.

He lights up a smoke. Bruce wide-eyed and in a panic. "Please. Look I'm just cutting through…I didn't see it…I mean I." The man grabs the bat with a firm grip.

It's clear he doesn't have anything to say. Bruce turns to run, but the man is a lot quicker, especially with an extra three-foot reach with his bat. *Cling*, Bruce catches the bat to the back of the head. Bruce watches the upcoming street, Amber Street; stupid Amber Street. He watches the cars zoom by while he goes black and falls to the ground. He lays unconscious in the middle of the alleyway.

Chapter 4
May 5th, 1998 (9:22 P.M.)

The prosecutor sits on his table and watches her every movement while Elizabeth goes through detail. Elizabeth shakes her head clear of the memories.

The prosecutor jumps up, "So you were working that night? The night that they brought Bruce in from this incident?"

"Yes."

"And how was that?"

"How do you think it was?"

Wilson stands up, "Your honor. He's badgering Miss Primrose. Clearly, that is uncalled for."

The judge looks down at the prosecutor. "Proceed."

The prosecutor looks at Elizabeth. "Well?"

She looks away from him and replies, "It hurt me to see him hurt. It hurt to know that I ran our date short. I mean, he could have been with me. And he wouldn't have got rolled into the hospital that night. Which in turn he wouldn't have turned into what he became."

The prosecutor turns around with a stern face. "What exactly did you mean by that?"

Elizabeth looks away and Bruce shoots through her memories.

The prosecutor steps closer, "What did you mean? Please remember you're under oath."

Elizabeth looks over everyone in her life that is there in that courtroom. There for her. She can see the others that are here for Bruce. "Well, after he got hurt, something turned off inside him…he turned numb and that was just the beginning. He became a monster."

"I see…tell us Miss Primrose. Why don't you go on and finish your story."

Elizabeth calms a little, "Well I was at the hospital that night he was wheeled in."

"What did you see?"

"He seemed okay. The ambulance brought him in, but he wasn't in shock. Well, confused if anything."

"Confused…continue."

***

Ambulance lights light up the street as the ambulance screams and takes a corner, pulling into the hospital's parking lot. It pulls in quick and up to a halt, then puts the reverse lights on and begins to back up to the E.R.'s doors. The heads up was already given to the staff of the hospital, so they all knew that the ambulance was on its way. A few nurses run out to help the trauma victim that just arrived at the hospital in the screaming ambulance.

Elizabeth and her crew powerwalk out of the hospital doors, straight up to the back of the ambulance. They push a wheelchair, following procedure very closely and not really knowing what to expect. The three nurses step back as the ambulance doors fly open. The medic in the back is smiling and there is a lot of laughter for a trauma emergency.

More far-off laughter comes from another medic that is riding in the back. Elizabeth, not sure what's going on exactly, still proceeds to scream orders.

"We need to get him to the E.R. room. It should already be set up and prepped for him to go in." Elizabeth gets cut off by her own emotion, pure emotion, which floods her once she sees who's laying on the gurney in the back of the ambulance. Elizabeth screams and leaps into the back of the ambulance.

"Bruce!"

Bruce seems okay, just in pain when she touches him. "Yeah, I'm okay, I'm okay. I was just telling Ralf here about… how does a penguin build a house?"

Bruce lays his head back, in pain, and Elizabeth gets a grin and replies,

"Igloos it together."

He smiles at her and feels a great deal of relief that she's there. "I guess I wanted to see you even more than what I thought." Elizabeth smiles and helps get him down out of the back of the ambulance.

Bruce goes to stand up and get out of the gurney. He attempts to get into the wheelchair by himself and the staff gets crazy and overdramatic. They stop him and practically carry him over to the wheelchair. He gets a kick out of them.

Once he gets in the wheelchair, Elizabeth grabs the handles on the back. "Thanks, guys. I'll take him from here." Elizabeth pushes him down the hallway.

"What on Earth happened to you? I was just with you not two hours ago."

"It happened really fast." Elizabeth wheels him down the hallway to a back room and yells at the doctors in the distance.

"I'm putting him in room 208." Bruce gets in his room and stands up and out of the wheelchair very slowly.

Elizabeth grunts for him, not sure if he's okay. He has dry blood running down his neck and down the back of his shirt. Elizabeth tries to comfort him.

"That shirt has blood on it. Here, take it off…and I do believe you need an x-ray."

"You got it. I got to see my dad tonight."

Bruce sits down on the bed and grunts and playfully smiles. "Is that how this happened?"

"You look real pretty in those…scrubs."

"You think so?"

Elizabeth smiles at him. He struggles to get his shirt off; Elizabeth rushes over to give him a hand.

"Slow down, here."

He struggles, and then the shirt flies off, in the process. Bruce grunts and gets dizzy eyed. He shakes it off and smiles at Elizabeth, and Elizabeth makes deep heartfelt eye contact with him. Bruce feels it too. "I'm glad you're here with me."

Elizabeth takes the shirt and puts it aside. "Me too," she replies to him.

"Here, change into that, and someone will be in to talk to you and take you down the hall for that x-ray." She throws him a gown.

Elizabeth goes to leave.

"Oh yeah, how *did* this happen?"

Bruce looks up and tries to explain the incident but looks off, confused. "There was a man and I…I wanted a shortcut. I'm sorry I'm not remembering it right."

***

Elizabeth goes back into Bruce's room after making a round. He sits there awaiting someone to push him to his next procedure. Elizabeth pushes the door open and sees him sitting in the wheelchair. She smiles at him. "Are you ready to go?" Bruce covers himself with the thin clothed gown and plays shy.

"I'm ready when you are." Elizabeth laughs at him. She walks behind him and proceeds out of the doorway and down the hall.

It only takes a second and they're at the first door to the x-ray room.

Bruce looks up and back at Elizabeth, "Really? That took us literally five seconds. I was sitting there for fifteen minutes. Sitting there with my gown flapping in the breeze."

Elizabeth pushes open the door which leads to the first x-ray room. Basically, resembles a large closet, with a large viewing window and a few computer monitors. It lets you see into the second x-ray room.

Elizabeth smiles politely at Miss Helms, the x-ray nurse. She looks back from one of the monitors; a young girl with thick glasses.

The glasses never seem to sit right on her face, and her jacket needs to be a few sizes smaller. Elizabeth wheels Bruce past her.

She stands up and tosses the candy bar aside, and smiles at her next patient. He gets wheeled through the next doorway with a push. The door swings open to a cold dark room. A cold table sits in the center of the second x-ray room.

Elizabeth wheels him up to the table. The door gets pushed open and Miss Helms comes in. Elizabeth looks down at Bruce, "Well I can't really be in here for this, but I'll be watching from the next room. I'll be waiting to take you back to your room when you're done."

***

The x-ray nurse, Miss Helms is with him in the x-ray room. Elizabeth watches on from the monitoring room. She helps Bruce onto the table and lays him flat, then leaves the room. Bruce looks over to Elizabeth through the window, in the next room.

He lays there and starts feeling a little dizzy. He adjusts himself on the cold table and then hears a faint noise. He looks over and Elizabeth gets a *buzz* from her pager. She looks in for a second and then runs off down the hall.

Bruce lies back and then has a loss of thought control, as he feels a sharp pain in the very back of his head. Bruce thinks it's the cut from where he was hit. It has to be; he got hit life-threateningly hard. The machine kicks on with a loud *buzz,* then a loud *hiss.*

Miss Helms watches her computer, as she reaches over blindly searching for the rest of her candy bar. She is watching on while taking shots of this; the next beautiful bone structure.

She comes back in the room where Bruce lies. "Okay, lie still for only a second longer."

Bruce agrees and lies still. "I just want a few more shots." She goes back into the next room to the computer, and for a second time the slight *hiss* and then the *buzz* kicks off.

The same routine Miss Helms looks at the pictures. Bruce lies back and feels a slight loss of breath. He doesn't know if it is the machine or the effect of getting hit in the head. He adjusts and looks back at the window, and Elizabeth is back standing by the doorway looking in.

Miss Helms makes her way back into the x-ray room where Bruce lies. She walks in and opens the door, excusing herself past Elizabeth.

Miss Helms walks in and sits Bruce up. "You can go back to your room, and we will let you know the results in a few minutes."

She waves to Elizabeth to come in; she comes into the room with a wheelchair. Miss Helms smiles at him as he gets off the cold table. Bruce, short of breath and cold, shakes off a slight head change. Elizabeth rolls up and helps him into the chair.

Bruce relaxes and for a second feels normal. "Now I'm looking good, rolling." Elizabeth gets a kick out of his sense of humor. She wheels him out of the room and down the hall.

Miss Helms takes the prints to the doctor. Bruce's new room is up a floor and down a hallway. Elizabeth doesn't mind whatsoever taking him the entire way.

Elizabeth pushes him through the hall. "I'm so happy it's nothing bad or fatal. I don't want anything to hurt you," she says with complete sincerity.

Bruce looks back at her. "Yeah, you're telling me. It all happened too fast, and I thought I was having a good night. Trust me. I don't want anything to hurt me either."

Elizabeth stops the chair and walks in front of him and kneels down. "I don't want anything to happen to you. I like you, and I don't want to see you hurt. What would Oscar and I do if something happened?"

She ends her rant and goes to keep pushing him but is quickly distracted by a group of nurses running toward them. Elizabeth's radio blows up with panic. They look at the nurses in confusion. A doctor runs up behind them with the x-rays in his hand and quickly interrupts, "This man needs to get to surgery quick!" He says this with pure panic, ending any form of conversation.

***

The x-rays get shoved up into the blinding tray of bright light. The main doctor walks up to the x-rays and looks them over once again, making sure he knows exactly what's about to happen. He's already in full operating gear. He holds his blue latex-gloved hands in the air, ready to go to work on the patient.

Bruce is cleaned up and in the operation room, still not sure what exactly is happening. The nurse is talking him through everything. "We are going to need you to get face down on the table. We aren't sure if we need to put you to sleep or not."

Bruce gets up from the wheelchair and looks at the trays of tools and all the machines. He gets slightly nervous. "I'm not sure what's going on, but I feel fine…just lie face down?"

"Yes, and I'm going to cover you and get you ready for surgery."

Bruce takes a deep, nerve-racking breath. "Okay." He lies down and stays still, waiting for the storm of doctors to come rushing in, which they are about to do.

The main doctor still continues to overlook the images in the back of the room. "I need to see exactly what we are working with. There is a slight fracture, a graze in the back of his head, and a slim needlelike object still embedded in the skull." The doctor goes a little numb.

"The object has slightly entered the hippocampus tissue of his brain." The doctor nods to his assistant and looks down at a file on the table. She opens it up, and he nods to turn the page. He gets closer to read it.

"No signs of trauma or hemorrhaging. The patient seems slightly dizzy. At most mild concussion, with a cut in the back of the head." The doctor chuckles a little and looks at the x-ray because what he sees is life-threatening.

He rushes off in a hurry with his posse to help Bruce. Bruce lies still on his stomach when the group of doctors comes in. He can hear their indistinct voices all around him. He feels very awkward, like a guinea pig.

They don't acknowledge Bruce at all; they only pay attention to his body. It feels uncomfortable – mostly rude. He lies still overhearing the conversation rapidly firing all around him.

"Anesthesia?"

"No, we need to do this now. And we need him awake. He's going to be fine; it won't take too long. Scalpel."

Bruce feels a pinch in the back of his head. He lets out a little grunt. The doctor puts the knife on the table. "Tweezers."

"Was he only dizzy? Did he have any confusion? Different speech patterns? Cerebral palsy? Anything out of the normal?"

"No, only the mild concussion symptoms; he has been really responsive."

"Okay, I'm going to need extra gauze. I'm not sure if there will be a mess or not when I take this out."

"What did you find?"

"He has something puncturing his brain…"

Bruce goes wide-eyed with pure concern over his wellbeing after hearing the conversation. The doctors and nurses still swarm him. He tries his best to stay still. He doesn't feel anything.

He closes his eyes tight and his heart rate shoots up. The doctor grabs metal clamps and digs to get to the tiny sliver. He has it, and with a small breath and a steady precise hand, he pulls the piece out of Bruce's skull. It's a thin, two and a half-inch piece of glass.

The doctor pulls it all the way out and Bruce feels a sharp spike of pain. The sharp spike of pain almost puts him in an unpermitted daydream. He wants to blackout then, like a damaged computer rebooting. He manages to come back to his original consciousness a small blood spout and they have it covered.

Bruce adjusts a little. "That hurt."

"Sir? Are you okay? Can you hear me?"

"Yes, of course."

"Do you feel okay?" The doctor throws the thin sliver on the spotless tray next to him. "We found something in your head. It most likely got lodged in there from the impact to the back of your head, but we got it out."

"Can I move now?"

"Yes. Can you?"

The doctor sits Bruce up and looks him over. "How do you feel?"

Bruce smiles and says, "I'm a little dizzy."

"Confused?"

"No. I have a headache, but I'm okay. I feel fine." Bruce looks to him, makes eye contact, and shows complete honesty.

The doctor smiles, pats him on the shoulder, and walks out of the room. "I'm happy you're okay. That was a close one. Nurse, stitch him up and then take the patient to his room and give him a second evaluation and CAT scan."

Bruce shakes it off; he felt a relief of pressure in his head. Now he just has a terrible headache. Bruce looks over to the table and sees the enormous sliver of glass they just pulled from his head.

He is speechless. A nurse comes over and begins to work on Bruce's head.

***

Bruce sits on the hospital bed with his feet hanging over. Elizabeth walks around the corner into the doorway with Bruce's clothes in her hands. Bruce sits in a gown on a hospital bed with his hair a mess and bandages across the back of his head. He sits up straight when he sees her.

She smiles back at him and Bruce goes about saying, "I guess I wanted to see you more than I thought."

With a smile, he laughs, but only a little. Elizabeth makes her way in and puts his clothes on the bed next to him. She replies ever so calmly, "I'm sorry you had to go through all this."

She grabs his hand and squeezes it. Then she says with a stern voice, "Well here are your clothes, and this shirt needs to be thrown away."

She points out the bloodstain running across the back of it.

Dr. Blankly walks in, and in a hurry, looks them over and interrupts by saying, "Well Mr. Garner. You seem okay. I would like to keep you overnight to make sure you're feeling well, but Miss. Primrose said you had wanted to go home?" Dr. Blankly stares down through his glasses at Bruce. Bruce looks over to Elizabeth and replies to the doctor, "Yes, I'm fine. I mean, if you think I'm okay?"

"Well, you appear okay."

"Well then, I'll be okay, I mean I feel fine and I'll have a personal nurse at my side in a few hours anyway, right?"

Bruce grabs Elizabeth's hand and the doctor shies away. "I see."

He goes to the counter and writes out a release for Bruce to go.

The doctor also writes a prescription and hands them over to Bruce. "You look fine, but I want you to take this and come back in one week for a checkup."

Bruce gets to his feet and grabs his clothes behind him. The doctor walks out, looking back at Bruce as he stands "…and watch your step."

The doctor exits and Elizabeth hugs onto Bruce and whispers in his ear, "I'm coming by after work later this morning. Go get some rest and be careful." Elizabeth gives him a kiss, then pushes him away and turns to go back to work.

Chapter 5
May 6ᵗʰ, 1998 (Early Morning)

Bruce walks to the fridge and pulls the door open. The Microwave blinks 4:23 A.M. Bruce is searching for a late-night snack and after a night like this, he needs it. He swings closed the door to the fridge after grabbing himself a drink and a piece of cheese.

He leans against the counter and opens the lid to his drink. He hopes he didn't make a mistake coming home after that awkward surgery. Bruce goes into thinking that maybe he should be at the hospital right now. Then the dark figure in the alley comes into his thoughts.

Bruce can't even remember what his face looked like. He tries to remember, but he gets incredibly dizzy. He sets down his drink in an abrupt state, grasps the counter, and shakes.

"Why did you do this to me?"

He has a sharp pain in his head. He takes a deep breath, then breathes again normally. Bruce looks back at the clock and it still blinks 4:23 A.M. He slowly touches the bandage covering his head. Oscar makes his presence known with a simple "meow."

Bruce calms, leans down, and pets the cat on the head. "What's up buddy? You hungry?"

Bruce looks over to the cat's bowl and sees it's picked at. His cat will not touch the rest. He's a picky ass. Bruce goes and grabs the bowl, chucking the remains in the garbage.

He walks over to the cabinet and grabs the bag of cat food.

***

Bruce walks back to his bathroom with a handful of changing clothes. He walks in and looks at himself in the mirror, sighs, and then throws his clothes on the toilet lid before turning on the shower. Bruce is better now; his mood is changing. He looks himself in the mirror and smiles over the mess that is called, Bruce.

He goes to change his bandages and stops. All he can see are these last twelve hours. It's as if he is having a small anxiety attack: Elizabeth leaving, my dad's home, the attack in a dark alley.

He tries to shake it off but instead gets aggressively angry. Bruce angrily attempts to continue his procedure with his bandages, only adding to the fire. He grabs his head bandage and starts trying to rip it off. He gets mad, then stops and leans on the sink, trying his best to calm himself down.

Taking one deep breath after another, Bruce looks at himself in the mirror with glazed-over eyes. A simple tear runs down his cheek.

"Today was a hard day." Bruce watches the tear and does the one thing he can do; he laughs.

He turns on the water, splashes it over his face, and goes back to cleaning himself up. The white sheets and large bed look like another world, a simple soft heaven. He crawls in, clean and ready to sleep. He is wearing new bandages and now just wants to be able to turn it all off the ability to let go and fall asleep.

Bruce lies there staring at the fan spinning above him. It's amazing how tired he is, but he still can't turn it off. He can't stop the thoughts of the day. He fights and is able to stop his thoughts only with a small force.

He tries to sleep. His head begins to throb and hurt with an instant headache. Bruce grabs his head bandages, thinking he might have put them on too tight. His head is throbbing.

He knows there is no way he can sleep like this; it's too much. He gets lightheaded lying down. Then a small force of energy comes from his chest. It sends a throbbing sensation right to the back of his head.

Bruce lies there and takes it all. It's a small seizure. It has to be, but then it calms. His head hurts, but he is able to catch his breath and he sits up. There is a new rush through him and he needs to walk off the pain and shock of how his body is feeling. He has to get up.

***

Bruce sits on the couch and watches TV with the bandage still across the back of his head. He is finally a lot more comfortable after such an event. He flicks the channel once again but gets an abrupt distraction from Oscar. The cat jumps up on the back of the couch and plays with Bruce's head bandage.

Bruce loosened up his bandage, believing that's what was causing him the throbbing pain. The cat plays with it for a second longer, then gets pulled down by Bruce. He pulls Oscar down on his lap, smiles, and feels once again at peace. The clock on the TV reads 6:37 A.M.

It seems like it's still dark outside, but it's only because the dark shades are completely drawn. Bruce reaches over, grabs a glass of water, and takes a sip while watching a comedy hour. He laughs out loud and, in the process, wakes Oscar, who is now purring on his lap. He flicks the channel but is interrupted.

There's a knock on the door. It throws off his sense of relaxation and comfort.

Bruce slowly moves Oscar and mumbles to himself, "Who is here at 6:40?"

He thinks it's Elizabeth, but can't be positive, because he knows she gets off at 7:00.

Bruce looks out the peephole, and sure enough, it's Elizabeth. He unlocks the door and swings it open. He smiles and then, with a stern voice asks, "Where is the key, I lent you?"

Elizabeth smiles, amazed he answered so quickly; she figured he would be out like a light.

"I think I left that key here on accident. You seem wide awake. Did you sleep?"

They walk into the living room, and Oscar makes himself seen to get some attention from

Elizabeth.

Bruce answers, "No. I got home and felt groggy, even dizzy. I felt like I wanted to sleep at first then I just didn't feel it. Why are you off so early?"

"I came by to make sure you're okay. I brought you something to help you sleep if you like."

Bruce walks away toward the couch, going to sit back down. He turns to face her while she closes the door. Elizabeth stands leaning up against the shut door, acting seductive toward Bruce. She pulls a needle and a small tube of liquid from her pocket. She walks toward him and places the medicine on the table. Then she walks over to him looks down at herself, and smiles.

She gets close to his lips and says, "This is something to help you sleep…and the doctor recommended the medicine…That's to help you sleep also."

***

The bed is so soft, and the beam of sunlight seems to warm and bounce off the white sheets. The sun's rays beam in straight up to Elizabeth's face. She looks like an angel, as the glow comes off as magical. She is wearing a beautiful white nightgown when she wakes up on this gorgeous day.

Elizabeth stretches out and feels the warmth and glow of the day, hoping to feel a soft, warm Bruce lying next to her, but her hand falls short. She shakes off the sleep and looks to the side of the bed. No one lays next to her. She rubs her eyes and forces them the rest of the way open.

Elizabeth sits up completely, and what she sees isn't warm or welcoming in any way. The other end of the room seems dark, with no light hitting it, and there's a shadow standing in the doorway. Bruce is standing, watching her sleep. Elizabeth sees Bruce staring at her in the doorway, and for some reason it makes her heart jump.

"Oh, you scared me. What are you doing awake?" She looks over to the clock and it reads 11:04 A.M. She looks back to Bruce and he's now a lot closer.

Bruce is standing off to the side of the bed in the corner of the room. He moves in quickly and still just stares. Once again, her stomach drops with his movement; she doesn't like it. It scares her.

Elizabeth looks around wondering if he is staring at something else, but she's the only thing there. Confused, she mutters, "Baby what are you doing? Did you sleep?"

Bruce moves a few steps closer into the warm light.

"A little, just long enough to actually fall asleep, you know? But I'm wide awake now," Bruce replies to her in a deep drifting voice. Elizabeth sits all the way up and gets on the defensive. She looks for her pants.

"Yeah. Well, how is your head? You might want to lie down for a bit longer; it's only been three hours, maybe three and a half. You weren't asleep long enough for that dose of medicine to really affect you."

Bruce walks around to the opposite side of the bed, sits down with his back to Elizabeth, and replies, "I fell asleep. I think I'm okay for a while."

"For a while?"

"It's awkward being in a body with no limits."

Elizabeth gets a cold chill down her spine. Her warm beautiful morning is getting very cold. She is not sure why this negative vibe is so strong.

She turns around to see him; he sits with his back to her: still and cold. Elizabeth sits at the edge of the bed and puts on her pants and shoes. She attempts to shake off the daze; she feels like she woke up in a different world. Bruce doesn't feel like the same man she went to sleep with this morning.

His vibe heightens her senses, putting her on guard. She puts on her clothes, almost in a panic. Bruce sits quietly and never faces Elizabeth.

Elizabeth gets on her shirt then says, "I need to go. I haven't even showered. You just rest and I'll come back in a few hours, okay?"

She stands up and turns around to see him. His bandage is loose, but his head looks fine. He sits quietly which is even stranger. It's not the positive Bruce that she knows.

Elizabeth, confused over his vibe and behavior, gets a tear in her eye. "Bruce? I'll come back…okay?" Bruce puts off a vibe of pure aggression and hate.

Elizabeth's sixth sense goes off and she wants to leave the apartment.

She goes for the door. "You sleep more and I'll be back. Bruce…call me if you need anything." Elizabeth looks back to him.

Sitting with his back to her as she leaves, he doesn't say a thing as she closes the door behind her.

***

Elizabeth sits crouched on the stand in awe over remembering the first morning. It scares her to remember that morning. Her tears roll, but that doesn't even come close to a resemblance of the panic she feels inside.

She looks out over the crowd and once again repeats what Bruce said, "It's awkward being in a body with no limits."

Elizabeth adjusts in her seat, obviously uncomfortable. "That's the first time he was there; he said that. 'It's awkward being in a body with no limits.'"

The prosecutor does what he does best, first only stares at Elizabeth and then with a stern voice says, "Ms. Primrose, what exactly did you give Bruce that morning when you went to see if he was indeed okay?"

"Zalaplon."

"Yes, and where did you get this Zalaplon?"

"Dr. Blankly. He gave it to me to give to Bruce to help him sleep. I assume he gave it to Bruce first, but maybe Bruce forgot to take it."

"Did Bruce use the drug?"

"Yes, but it only worked for a couple of hours, and the dose I gave him was the dose prescribed. Should have put him to sleep for eight to ten hours easily."

"A couple of hours? What is that two, four?"

"Three and a half. And when I woke, he seemed wide awake like he wasn't on anything."

"He was fine other than the 'creepy vibe?'"

"Yeah," Elizabeth replies with deep thought in her eyes, confused just as much as the prosecutor.

The prosecutor struts around and tries to make sense of it.

"Okay, so let me get my head around all this. He gets hurt and asks to be released from the hospital? And in this entire time, he says he feels fine?"

Elizabeth seems off-put by the question, straightens up, and answers honestly, "Yes, he said he was fine from the surgery. I thought he was fine all the way up to the morning I went to him and all the way until he woke up. He woke up odd. Not odd in a physical form, but it wasn't him. His physical self was fine, but his personality was off."

"After you left that morning, did you try to call him?"

"Yes."

"And?"

"He didn't answer…"

"How often did you try? I mean, you had to of tried more than once. I mean, he was your boyfriend. He could have been hurt."

"Yes, of course, I called more than once. I also called later that afternoon and nothing. I tried again that night – nothing. The next day – nothing."

"Why didn't you go to him? Check his apartment? You made it clear in your story you had a key."

"I left the key there, and I only realized I had left it at Bruce's house when I went there later that day! You don't think I tried to help him? I was worried about him."

Elizabeth puts her head in her hands and begins to speak out loud, "It wasn't until the fourth day that I got a very disturbing text message from Bruce."

The prosecutor lights up in a sense and cuts her off, "Ah! Yes, the text that read…" The prosecutor runs back to his notes. It only takes a second and the prosecutor has it in his hand.

He is somehow instantly and amazingly organized, and he continues on. "He writes, and I quote, 'I'm going to the hospital. I haven't slept. I need you there with me…need sleep. That is what he wrote?"

Elizabeth replies to the prosecutor, "Yeah, then before I could respond to his text, he was calling me on the phone. He was panicky, scared, paranoid, crying, and sobbing, then shouting out loud."

"What else was he doing while on the phone with you?"

"Shouting. He was driving himself to the hospital, so I tried to keep him on the phone until he got there."

Elizabeth once again breaks into tears. The judge waves to his attendant to get a glass of water. The prosecutor carries on and begins again.

"Now he said, 'I haven't slept, I need sleep?' What did he mean by that?"

Chapter 6
May 10ᵗʰ, 1998 (I Can't Sleep)

The hospital sits at the edge of town, on a quiet hill. Elizabeth is on the ass end of her shift. She takes a breather from the numerous things the night shift nurses have to do. She walks out onto the second level balcony. The balcony looks over the hospital's parking lot. She makes her way outside to watch the sun come up. She looks at her watch 6:43 A.M. She goes over the thought of all the duties that still need to be done, before her shift change. There's not much, but she's ready to go home this dim morning.

She stops and leans on the railing and thinks. It has been a rather peaceful night. A buzz goes off from in her white-jacket pockets. It's her cell phone.

She looks over the screen and it's a text message, and the alert reads, 'Bruce.'

Elizabeth opens the phone and begins to read the message, "I'm going to the hospital, haven't slept." She stops in the middle of reading the text because her phone rings loud and clear. Now it's Bruce calling.

She answers the phone. "Hey."

"I need help, I'm coming to you."

***

The night staff gets ready for the arrival of a panicked patient. A patient that is going to be driving himself up to the hospital at any moment. A nurse stands to watch. She was given the vehicular description and was told to yell as soon as Bruce shows.

The silver truck shows up to the hospital's parking lot. Bruce drives up to the front E.R. entrance and stops with a halt. The Nurse on the lookout sees the vehicle and it matches the description. She calls out to everyone down the hallway.

"He pulled up! Come on everyone, let's go."

A brigade of nurses come around the corner unified as they rush past the lookout and out the doors. Elizabeth runs out behind all of them, with Dr. Blankly next to her.

Bruce is still on the phone glued to Elizabeth's ear, but all she hears now is his heavy breathing. The vehicle is stopped. They all run to the curb. Bruce sits in the vehicle, calm after he pulled up, not in any rush. Bruce looks over to them and then manages to put his truck in park.

His door swings open, and he puts his leg out. Everyone sees him, but in some way looking to Elizabeth for any form of command.

Bruce unbuckles his belt and gets out like every thing's alright. Elizabeth not sure how to take control of this situation; simply because of how confused she is.

She closes her phone. He seems okay. Bruce also calmly hangs up the phone with Elizabeth. He walks around his truck. He looks okay, maybe a bit unbalanced.

Elizabeth walks up to him concerned. He moves up and gives her a hug. The team still out and surrounding him, you can see confusion in their eyes. They almost start to joke a little. He calmly sits in a wheelchair that was rolled out for him. Under the understanding that he was hurt.

Bruce looks up to Elizabeth with a smile. The crew calms and thinks he's joking. A snicker comes across some of their faces. Dr. Blankly looks down at Elizabeth, not sure how to take it.

"Give him an observation booth let's look at him."

One of the nurses goes to push him in and Elizabeth stops him from touching the wheelchair.

Elizabeth half tired, and is trying to maintain a good eye on her position at the hospital, takes control. "Go get back to work. I'll take care of him. Thank you, guys."

The crew members go back in and the one nurse lets go of the chair and shrugs his shoulders walking back inside. Elizabeth stands in front of Bruce; Bruce keeps his smile. Elizabeth not sure how to take him and this off-putting grin. She has to at least understand.

"Bruce are you okay? What is this? You're scaring me, I mean what is this phone call all about?" Bruce shakes his head. He has a dazed look.

He goes to respond but stops. Elizabeth stalls for a second being patient then, "Bruce!"

Bruce looks to her with a simple reply, "I'm happy to see you."

"Is this a fucking joke? You had me freaking out!"

"I'm happy to seyyyooouuu…" Bruce slightly stutters, and slightly slobbers the last part of the sentence; he just repeated.

This catches Elizabeth completely off guard, "Bruce are you feeling okay?" She asks him with great concern.

Bruce lunges up out of the chair stands straight up and in her face. Naturally, this abruptness makes Elizabeth jump back about five feet. She looks around in shock then looks to the complete stranger standing in front of her. It's not him.

Bruce stands and spouts out sentences. "Waits for the man!" He shouts out loud.

This makes Elizabeth's heart thump loud. Elizabeth stands scared as Bruce yells off a little more.

"The one who might get him. What he needs to pass and let another...force enter this body!"

Bruce lets off a raspy yell, it sends chills up Elizabeth's back. Bruce loses his wind and sits back down. A male nurse and an older gentleman walk in the lobby, coming out of the front entrance doors. The male nurse is a new worker at the hospital, and he already has to witness this extravaganza.

Little does this new nurse know, that he's standing right next to an amazing man, Dr. Zazio, a miracle maker, a Neurologist. He's one of the best in the studies of the human brain and habits.

This amazing doctor, Dr. Zazio looking over and criticizing the hospital, but right now this situation with Bruce and Elizabeth has called out to get his complete attention. Bruce adjusts his face then grins at Elizabeth. Elizabeth is speechless, she knows something is terribly wrong. She looks around the hospital parking lot.

The nurse walks over to them slowly, not sure what exactly is going on. He gets closer and sees Elizabeth speechless with tears in her eyes. Bruce sits grinning. He has a locked stare on her. It looks like she's even a little scared to move.

The nurse gets closer. "Is everything okay? Miss. Primrose?"

Elizabeth snaps back into it and walks behind Bruce and he puts his feet up in the wheelchair. Elizabeth begins to push him into the hospital.

Wheels him past the nurse and a somewhat in awe Dr. Zazio. Elizabeth pushes him into the lobby. The light from inside the hospital shows a slight blood trail on the back of Bruce's head and down his shirt. Blood from where the piece of glass was once inserted.

***

Elizabeth pushes aside a curtain that divides the hospital room. It opens up to the other end of the exam room. She pushes the curtain further over. Elizabeth turns around and looks at Bruce sitting in the hallway.

She goes over and rolls Bruce into the room. Dr. Zazio waltzes from around the corner and from down the hall. He watches Elizabeth roll him into the room. Elizabeth stops the chair next to the bed.

She's confused over Bruce's actions entirely. "Do you need help?" Bruce looks back and up to her with his head arched backward from where he sits. His head goes limp and hangs down.

Elizabeth feels out of her comfort zone but helps Bruce off the chair and onto the bed. He chuckles a little when she lifts him, and it raises the hair on her arms. He tenses up making things more difficult while Elizabeth fights with him. She feels frustrated and confused, but he feels so weak and fragile like he wants to collapse right this second.

Once, she helps him off the chair; he instantly falls unto the bed. He looks like he wants to pass out right at that very moment, but instead of going out; his eyes pop wide open. Like someone turned on a light deep inside him. Elizabeth watches in a slight shock.

She feels sorry for him. She shakes her head in panic. She turns around to see Dr. Zazio watching them from across the hall. Elizabeth walks over and pulls the door closed.

Elizabeth keeps a firm grip on the handle then turns around to Bruce. She jumps and gets a little uncomfortable. Bruce is sitting up and is staring straight at her. He doesn't blink or say a word. He just smiles.

Elizabeth looks at him confused, but she's instantly distracted when the door bursts open behind her. Dr. Blankly comes rushing in from the hallway. Dr. Blankly leaves the door wide open and makes his way around the bed, to a delusional Bruce.

Elizabeth walks back over to the door, closes it off from the morning commotion in the hallway.

Bruce sits up and in a raspy voice greets the doctor, "Doc. You're looking mighty fine today."

Elizabeth looks at him terrified in a sense, maybe it's because she knows this man, and he isn't Bruce. Elizabeth wants to cry.

She puts her hand over her mouth as Bruce comes in and out of collected consciousness Dr. Blankly watches him. He has no motor skills at all; simply observing.

"Bruce? Bruce are you in there? Talk to me if you can hear me." Bruce tries to reply, but only mumbles off.

He doesn't make any sort of sense at all with his words. Dr. Blankly is distracted by Elizabeth's grasp on his shoulder. He looks back at her and remembers that these two know each other. They even might have been a thing.

He looks up to Elizabeth. Bruce continues to ramble on. She has her hand over her mouth almost in shock. Dr. Blankly in a slight panic gets up from his seat and walks around Elizabeth.

He puts his hand on her shoulder comforting her. He swings open the door behind her. Elizabeth's eyes are glued on Bruce.

Dr. Blankly yells out loud, "Nurse Judy? Nurse Judy?"

An old, stern Nurse Judy, walks around the corner. She struts her way toward the doorway. Dr. Blankly comes back in the room and then Nurse Judy comes from around the corner. She looks over Elizabeth's shoulder and Dr. Blankly nods to her to take Elizabeth out of the room.

Nurse Judy looks at Elizabeth and slowly calms her and turns her out of the room. The door is left swinging open and Dr. Blankly once again yells out loud. "Nurse? We need to get 10cc of zolpidem or anything with benzodiazepines in here with a prepping needle."

A second nurse comes in from the hall with a table of supplies, needles, and medicines. The nurse doesn't have what he needs on the tray at least he doesn't have what the doctor called out for. The nurse looks for a second longer then rushes out of the room to go grab the benzodiazepines. Dr. Blankly looks Bruce over and puts up one finger, then shines a light in Bruce's eyes.

Elizabeth steps in for a second. She's still a little shaken, but mentions, "He has a small stream of blood that appeared to have come from his head, in the back."

Dr. Blankly slowly moves Bruce forward and sits him up.

He looks at the back of his head. He turns to Elizabeth, "He said, 'he hadn't slept from that day?'"

Elizabeth catches her breath while making an attempt to make sense of all this. "The day after that morning…oh god, four days."

Elizabeth manages to mutter out. Bruce rambles off, "I need to tell you all sooo much sooo…"

Elizabeth's jaw drops and she turns around and immediately leaves the room. Dr. Blankly looks back and watches her storm away concerned.

She can't be in there with him being this way. Elizabeth feels her face get red and her eyes water up. She can't help. She can only put her head in her hands while she stands on the other side of the doorway.

A soft touch comes from her colleague as he returns with a few new bottles of medicine. Nurse Judy comes back around and grabs the Medicine from him and walks toward Bruce's room. Dr. Blankly looks at Bruce and Bruce just stares at the Doctor. Dr. Blankly's stomach drops a little.

Nurse Judy storms in closing the door behind her. She hands Dr. Blankly the medicines, and he swings the table over and grabs a needle. The tiny bottle reads zolpidem. Dr. Blankly wipes Bruce's arm down. "Now it's time for you to feel better and get some sleep."

Dr. Blankly pricks him with the needle and pushes the plunger.

He continues on his rant. "Now, Bruce this should hit you really fast, so I need you to lay comfortably back." Dr. Blankly and Nurse Judy lie Bruce back on the bed and then stand over him.

They wait for a minute or so, but Bruce's eyes don't shut. Bruce has no response. Yet Dr. Blankly with complete confidence nods in approval and looks to Nurse Judy. "Watch him, when he goes out, let me know and then we'll get a blood sample."

Dr. Blankly paces back and forth a little more and plays it off that he's not confused. Deep down Dr. Blankly knows any other man would have been knocked out completely, in seconds flat. Dr. Blankly walks to the open door and out of the room. He looks back and watches Bruce eyeball him the entire time, still wide awake.

Dr. Blankly shakes it off and closes the door behind him. His heart must have skipped a beat. He gets the file off the door, then walks down the hall. He walks and looks over the file, but pauses when he sees Dr. Zazio watching him from down the hallway.

Dr. Zazio is fixed on Dr. Blankly even though Dr. Zazio is engulfed in his own conversation with another member of the hospital. Dr. Zazio smiles at him as Dr. Blankly makes an abrupt right, into his office.

***

Dr. Blankly sits in his office for a few minutes; even goes as far as to get a little nervous. He opens up a portfolio on his desk and then closes it immediately afterward. He sits back with his hands over his head, distressed, waiting for

Nurse Judy to come in his office, any second with news on Bruce. Fifteen minutes or so later.

Dr. Blankly looks at his watch then gets up and looks down the hallway at the room. Finally, a small amount of relief. He sees, Nurse Judy, open the door and walks out, toward his office. Dr. Blankly goes out and meets her in the middle of the hallway.

"Already asleep? I knew a simple dose would."

Nurse Judy shakes her head, "No."

She makes eye contact with a concerned look spread across her face.

She tries to reply, "No, He's still awake. He hasn't even seemed to blink or close his, um…eyes."

Dr. Blankly looks away and around completely confused; unable to even put it into words.

The nurse continues, "But I'm out here coming to tell you, that his eyes are watering terribly. But he's not showing any form of emotions."

Dr. Blankly gives a concerned look to her and they walk toward Bruce's room.

Nurse Judy continues, "So I don't think its tears."

They walk past the hallway and Dr. Blankly sees Dr. Zazio standing alone, and stares down the hallway watching them.

They go in the room, Dr. Blankly pulls back the curtain to see Bruce still awake. Nurse Judy was right. He has something coming from his eyes. Dr. Blankly leans closer, wide-eyed.

"Bruce? Are you alright?" Bruce's eyes roll toward him and they make eye contact.

He turns his head and looks to him in a jerking motion.

Bruce makes them jump; catches both of them off guard.

Dr. Blankly thinks quickly. "Give me a cotton swab from there." He points at the tray in the corner of the room, and Nurse Judy jumps to command.

She hands it over. Dr. Blankly with precision swipes Bruce's cheek. He gets some of the gooey substance. Dr. Blankly hands the swab back to the nurse.

"Have that tested. It's not tears." The nurse runs off to go get it done. Dr. Blankly turns away from Bruce and feels a chill come up his spine.

He looks back in deep thought and looking at the gooey liquid. It makes his stomach drop and he says under his breath.

"I think it's the medicine." Bruce is still wide awake as another nurse enters the room.

"Do you need anything? Dr. Blankly?"

He looks back at her confused but determined. "Yeah, we need morphine in here with the same setup. I'm not messing around…on the fly come on let's go!"

Bruce keeps his eyes on the doctor then he reaches up and wipes his right eye. Dr. Blankly turns to Bruce, "Bruce? Can you hear me?"

Bruce looks at his hand in awe with the goo on it.

He turns to the doctor. "Yes. I can hear you." His voice is very off-putting deep and dark. Bruce slams his hand on the bed and wipes it off on the sheets, smiling.

The nurse comes back in with the morphine and another needle. Dr. Blankly is non-hesitant and grabs Bruce's arm. He wipes it off, and then grabs the needle from the nurse.

He looks at Bruce, and then a small pinch. The needle goes in.

The medicine he gives him should put him down instantly…but it doesn't. Dr. Blankly watches him with patients, then stands and paces back and forth. Bruce coughs a little then his eyes go shut. Dr. Blankly gets very happy and surprised, but no time to wait.

He turns to the nurse to give more commands, but gets cut off by a horrifying scream! Bruce yells out loud in multiple tones. His back is arched up in pain and agony.

Elizabeth hears Bruce's startling cries all the way from the break room. She sits frozen in fear; with a death grip on her candy bar that she was using to comfort herself. Dr. Blankly jumps onto

Bruce confused about what to do. He tries not to hold him to tight. It might be a seizure.

Dr. Blankly looks to the nurse that is standing in shock. "Nurse? Nurse! We need to move him to another room. Okay, I'll need you to get a gurney and…"

Dr. Blankly stops and looks at Bruce's clothes, they're soaked in liquid.

Bruce stops and looks both of them in the eye, and blabs on somewhat docile. "When you can't clean the body of the entity. The entity feels it. In its own ability to tear down the walls holding it in. This is mine."

Bruce falls over and twitches. Elizabeth comes rushing around the corner to the entrance of the room. She still holds her candy bar, tight in her grasp. Dr. Blankly looks over to her, winded and scared.

Bruce gags and sits up choking! He flings himself back onto the bed. Dr. Blankly flips him over on his stomach. Bruce is soaking wet.

Bruce stops choking and begins to puke on the floor. Elizabeth is pale and motionless witnessing all of this. More nurses come running in moving her aside so they can bring in a gurney and more assistance. She leans back up against the hospital wall looking in at Bruce, from across the hallway.

Elizabeth can't take it, as tears roll down her face. She covers her mouth and runs away. Dr. Zazio walks up with a small strut, watching her run off down the hallway. He leans up against the wall in the exact same spot that Elizabeth stood simply to see what she saw.

He looks in and sees Bruce wet and staring off to the ceiling after being flipped back over. Dr. Blankly comes out of the room, dumbfounded and even more concerned. A nurse comes out of the room behind Dr. Blankly.

The nurse is straight-faced. Dr. Blankly leans over to him. "Move him to the I.C.U. ward and I'll come down in a bit."

The nurse goes to leave, but Dr. Blankly stops him and grabs his sleeve. "Tell Nurse Judy to find Elizabeth."

The nurse nods and walks back into the room and closes the door behind him. Dr. Blankly stares off in a daze, but a deep voice gets his attention. "Looks like a tough night. Tough issues?" Dr. Blankly looks Dr. Zazio over. The look on Dr. Blankly's face explains exactly how he feels about the situation. Dr. Zazio is more curious then sympathetic.

Dr. Blankly looks over to the doctor and asks, "Do you know anything about sleep patterns?"

"Oh yes, they are recently one of my deepest specialties." Dr. Zazio with pure confidence continues on his brigade. He wants to learn more about his new find. This once bystander just became a very intimidating doctor that sees what he wants.

Dr. Zazio's smile drops, and he gets close to Dr. Blankly. Too close for comfort.

He has completely stopped being casual. He looks him over then asks, "How long has he been awake?"

Dr. Blankly sighs and looks at him in confusion and defeat. They walk down the hallway to finish their conversation.

***

The prosecutor stands at Elizabeth's side watching her every word. He walks toward his side of the courtroom. He's sly, struts with his hands in his pockets. He interrupts her with a question. "So, Dr. Zazio took Bruce to his hospital?"

Elizabeth takes a deep breath trying her hardest to make it all clear for everyone. She reaches out and once again adjusts the microphone to her liking.

She scoots up closer with a response, "Yes. It was Dr. Zazio that took him down there to that...that place. What you would call an asylum, much less a hospital." The prosecutor rubs his nose and forehead while looking over his notes.

He holds out a small stack of papers in his hand. He walks up to Elizabeth, "Let me say you hate, Dr. Zazio? Why? And if you hate him, then why did you go with them?

It says right here that you didn't hesitate and you just jumped on his bandwagon."

"I didn't know the man, then. I basically went for Bruce. I went for him, and I was somewhat lucky, if you want to even call it that. They needed another nurse because Dr. Zazio was shorthanded taking on another patient. So, I volunteered."

"How was Bruce when he arrived at the hospital? Had he slept?"

At this point, the prosecutor is actually trying to be understanding.

Elizabeth replies to his question with complete honesty. "Well at this point he hadn't slept for five days. That's one hundred and twenty hours awake and not since the morning he woke up with me. He was out of it, even his body didn't know what to do. I don't think Bruce's conscience knew what to do or what was going on. I honestly thought he was just going to die if he didn't go to sleep."

"How was the state of Dr. Zazio's hospital when you arrived…Hospital Necropolis?"

"I'm not sure…cold. Cold, with a nervous vibe attached. I don't really remember the opening of the front door, but I remember clearly going down those stairs. At the beginning and even after we got there, it was obvious there was a negative vibe in the place. Sadly, it was Bruce that brought it down there."

"Cold?"

"Yeah, that's clear in my memory."

"The vibe? You said, 'Bruce brought it there?'"

"Yes."

"How?"

"I don't know what he became, but it was evil. That day was like no other. It wasn't him." The courtroom is in complete silence and the tension is extremely thick.

The prosecutor catches his own breath and quickly calms himself. He continues with the allegations. He turns and walks back to his side of the courtroom. He throws the papers down.

The prosecutor remembers a clear part of her story and brings it back up. "You said, 'you left.'"

"It was hard for me. To see him like that."

"But you still went to Dr. Zazio's hospital?"

"Yes, I cared for Bruce. I thought he would be more comfortable with me close by. I don't know, I was hoping he would just snap out of it. But he couldn't go to sleep."

The prosecutor pulls out more papers, and with a stern strut brings them up to the judge. "Now it says on those papers that he was clean. Nothing to keep him up or awake?"

"No. We gave him so much to put him to sleep, but his body."

Elizabeth tries her hardest to explain how quick Bruce's body forced the prescriptions out of his system.

She continues, "His body didn't take any of it. He wasn't having a response of any kind to anything."

"Yet, in the paper, the evidence says he was clean of everything that would keep him up?" The prosecutor replied.

"Keep him up? Of course not. We wanted to put him to sleep. But his body rejected everything, instantly."

"Okay, at this point he's at one hundred and twenty hours, awake? How did the body act without sleep for those straight five days?"

"Well, at first it was more of him not being able to control his body. He would lose the feeling in one-half of himself. Then at one point, he would fall over, but still, be wide awake. It was too much to watch him fall, especially when…when he stopped feeling the pain."

Elizabeth looks over her peers, and with a shaken voice tries to continue.

Chapter 7
May 11ᵗʰ–13ᵗʰ, 1998
(Hospital Necropolis)

Dr. Zazio sits large at the far end of a long table. He sits with his arms arched back and stretched over his head. He looks like if he could lift his feet up and put them on the table, he would. He gazes out the window and has a relaxed look on his face, as if he is in deep thought.

Then another question interrupts Dr. Zazio's thought once again.

"If it's alright with you, I want to come along to help out. Dr. Blankly said you were shorthanded so…" Elizabeth speaks loudly, trying to make her point while she sits calmly across the table from him.

She gets interrupted by Dr. Zazio, who adjusts himself, and mockingly leaning in forward to hear her better. Two women and one man sit on both sides of the table. Dr. Zazio sits staring straight at Elizabeth, not blinking and appearing very off-putting.

Elizabeth continues, "Dr. Blankly said you were shorthanded and I would like a temporary transfer to come along and help out with patient Bruce Garner in your hospital."

Dr. Zazio nods and looks around the table at his staff, making eye contact with a simple smile and chuckle. "Well you see, we are shorthanded and if you can get the transfer, I find it works better with the patients if someone close to them is there with them. In Bruce's case, having you around could be a great benefit." Elizabeth smiles, hoping she will get to be with Bruce, but her thought is quickly interrupted because Dr. Zazio wasn't finished.

"But it could be a complete disaster considering his state of mind. Will being around him in that state of mind, seeing what he is becoming…will that affect you or the quality of your work? Because I have three other patients that need attending to, almost in the same way as Bruce, and they're all also in very special conditions. I would need your full attention and support. I will and so will your team."

Elizabeth tries to keep her head up along with her character. "I don't think, being around Bruce will have any effect on my professional work as a nurse."

Dr. Zazio looks at her with a straight face for a minute. He leans back in his chair, "Well, Ms. Primrose, I think having an extra hand won't hurt."

Elizabeth smiles widely, then turns to the others at the table, nods, and smiles. Dr. Zazio continues, "Three other nurses, like yourself, will be counting on you; Miss. Walleton and Nurse Serana."

Elizabeth flashes another beautiful smile at the two nurses sitting next to each other.

Then, from the other side of the table, the one jolly man waves hi to Elizabeth, wearing a huge smile. Dr. Zazio points out the obvious. "…And of course, Brett is our other nurse."

Elizabeth smiles back politely.

Brett is anxious to get introduced and already piping off. "It's great to meet you. I really hope this all works out."

Dr. Zazio once again tries to continue but gets cut off by Brett whispering to Elizabeth. "Oh, sorry about your boyfriend."

Dr. Zazio shakes his head slightly. "Thank you, Brett. We also have a second doctor, Dr. Holden. He can't be here today, but considering these circumstances, he will get to meet you soon…oh, and of course, Simon the security guard. He's just the burly type with not too much to say, a lot of grunts and whatnot, but he can't be here today either."

Elizabeth smiles at her new team and replies, "Thank you, Dr. Zazio. I will work very hard for all of you and for these patients."

Dr. Zazio once again leans back and puts his hands over his head, "Let's say…Wednesday you will start." Elizabeth takes a deep breath, relieved in a sense, but she still has a deep fear stored away of what's to come.

***

Wednesday comes faster than Elizabeth planned. She's nervous and still scared for Bruce not to mention having to deal with such a serious situation with a group of strangers. Elizabeth pulls up to the address given to her by Dr. Zazio: an old lot on the outside of town, about a twenty-minute drive from their local hospital. Elizabeth pulls up to a tall wire fence with barbwire along the top and cameras on the far corners.

The fence is holding a tall gate, while it guards a small building in the middle of a ten-acre field. The tiny building looks like maybe one large room, or two. Elizabeth pulls up to the gate, facing inward. She looks at the tiny building, takes off her shades, and incomplete doubt, she knows this can't be the right place.

She puts her car in park and starts looking for the directions that were given to her by Dr. Zazio. In a frantic search, Elizabeth knocks the paper with the directions onto the floorboard of her car. She sits back up and goes to unfasten her safety belt, but stops. A camera turns and glares at Elizabeth.

She can see another camera on the corner of the gate turn her way also. Elizabeth looks over the fence and notices the inside gate has a sign on it, "Hospital Necropolis."

Elizabeth's doubt quickly fades away; she's certain now after reading the sign out loud

"Yep, this has to be the place." She unbuckles her seat belt, but it puts up a fight. She's tired and her mind is drained, but at least she looks wide-awake. She gets out of the car and walks up to the gate and waves her arms.

She looks at the camera and yells out loud, "Hello!" The closer she gets, the more she sees the extremes of the security surrounding this place, and it makes her concerned. She gets rattled by a loud buzz. Then the gate begins to slide aside.

She looks back up to the camera and smiles, then gets back in her car and throws it in drive. Her car pulls inside the gate, and once her car clears, the gate closes behind her.

She watches in the rearview as the barbwire fence closes her in. She is ready to meet up with Dr. Zazio as she drives up to what is supposedly a hospital.

Simon, the guard, opens the door to the entrance of the building. Elizabeth casually walks in and smiles. "I assume, you're Simon?" Simon attempts to give her his best smile after the giant of a man closes the door behind her.

"Yes, that would be me." The first room is a simple security room. Simon points to the wall of hung-up coats.

"Dr. Zazio likes it if you leave all of your personal belongings here."

Elizabeth smiles and hangs up her coat and throws her sunglasses in the coat's pocket after she hung it up. Simon opens another door and goes through, taking the lead while Elizabeth follows. Elizabeth looks around, still a little concerned by the size of the place. Elizabeth tries to talk to Simon.

"I don't see how it's possible to look after three other patients, not even including Bruce Garner, in these tight conditions." Elizabeth gets through the door and looks around. She's been taken to a lounge of some sort; clearly, the two rooms she has already been in take up a little more than half of this tiny building, and she's sure the restroom takes up the rest. Simon just chuckles and goes around to another hallway, back past the soda machine in the back of the lounge.

Elizabeth follows, and then once again Simon makes another quick right. Simon stops and points to another right turn. He stands and smiles at Elizabeth, "Everyone is right around the next corner. I have to stay up here, but you can go on."

Elizabeth looks and goes forward, a little nervous. She looks back at Simon, and he still holds his hand outward, pointing toward the turn. She laughs nervously and continues on. Elizabeth curiously looks around the corner, and to her surprise, a flight of stairs emerges that dive deep into the earth.

The staircase is wide, with a ramp on one side and a railing on the other. Elizabeth's eyes are trying to dilate so she can see. She takes a deep breath and proceeds down the staircase made of cement. She searches for the railing for support.

She finds it and takes a few steps down. Luckily, there is a faint light showing at the bottom. She looks down toward the light in the distance. It's really dark and hard to see anything in front of her at all.

If it wasn't for the faint light in the distance, she would be lost in the darkness. A dark figure appears at the bottom of the stairs. It's a dark figure that is overpowering and blocking her guiding light. Elizabeth gets on guard and slows her pace.

A familiar voice echoes through the air as Dr. Zazio calls out, "Elizabeth? Did you find the place okay?"

The figure becomes more visible the more steps she takes down the stairs and the more her eyes dilate to the dim-lit hallway that they now stand in. Dr. Zazio waits for her, then casually places his hand out to help her down the final steps.

"It's lovely to see you again and I'm glad you got here safe."

Elizabeth adjusts herself to the cold of the hospital, "Thank you, Doctor. So, this is it? This is where we will treat Bruce?"

"Yes, welcome to Hospital Necropolis." Dr. Zazio smiles, then begins to walk forward down the hall. He puts his hands behind his back and slowly paces, with Elizabeth following behind. Dr. Zazio shows her the hospital and describes the hospital for more of what it is.

Elizabeth follows, looking forward to this, but it's still not what she had ever expected. The concrete that floods the underground hospital is cold and seems to hold no place for even the slightest comfort. The walls and vibe of the hospital are unique, being built around the thirties. Rows of bright lights tower overhead, all the way down the wide hallway.

Dr. Zazio thinks for a second, turns around, looks at Elizabeth, and then addresses his hospital, "This is the main hallway. All the way down and on the left are the laboratories and examination rooms. On the right are the patients. There were only three, but now the last room at the end of the hall is set up for Mr. Garner."

They continue walking down the hall and the smell begins to get very musky; it is almost hard to breathe. Elizabeth feels the overwhelming vibe of this place but forgets all these things the second she hears a diabolical scream.

The scream has such velocity, it seems to shake the lights hanging from the ceiling. Elizabeth jumps back a few feet. She's actually calm inside, not scared. She's used to the screams of patients, but this time it is clear she was caught off guard.

Dr. Zazio keeps calm, and with his hands still placed behind his back, he walks up to the first door on his right. A steel door is shut and latched tight, and it's clearly where the scream came from. Dr. Zazio calmly looks in the window built into the door. Nurse Serana is sitting with a young, skinny man.

Serana sits next to him in a chair that is placed in the middle of the room. Dr. Zazio watches on for a second then looks away shaking his head in confusion. "Robert, twenty-six and frail, also with self-inflicted wounds."

"What's wrong with him?" Dr. Zazio continues, "A schizo sadly. His darkest delusion is that someone else is cutting and hurting him. He named it, Spingolia."

Elizabeth is intrigued to see the patient and quickly peeks in the window. Dr. Zazio turns to continue on down the hall. Elizabeth is a little relieved. She's been extremely curious about the actual range of diversity in the medical field that Dr. Zazio has a specialty in.

Elizabeth watches the young man, Robert, through the window. Robert sits in the corner of the room, not moving or saying anything to Serana. Elizabeth watches him shake in fear. She's relieved he's stopped shouting.

Then out of the blue, he makes eye contact with her.

Elizabeth holds her own and doesn't shy away or show any form of weakness. She then turns and follows Dr. Zazio down the hall. A few paces and once again, she is at Dr. Zazio's side.

He stops in front of another door. This door is a lot more advanced and high-tech than any of the other doors in the hallway. Elizabeth looks around him at the dimly lit hallway. She notices the only other high-tech door is the one that sits behind him.

The doors sit across from each other. Elizabeth hugs her notes tight while comparing the two doors. "That's one hell of a door." Elizabeth looks in the window.

Dr. Zazio gets a small laugh and moves to the side and opens a keypad.

He replies to Elizabeth, "Yes, it is. You see when you have to keep something in like a virus or a monster." Dr. Zazio smirks a little and continues on with the keypad.

Elizabeth looks to the door across the hall. "And that one?" Dr. Zazio turns around to see what she's talking about.

"Oh no. That door isn't as advanced. That's our laboratory room."

Dr. Zazio finishes up with the keypad and then the door unlatches and opens up. Elizabeth steps back and Dr. Zazio opens the door, going inside. The first door was only the beginning. He reveals to Elizabeth a small corridor room.

It's an incubation chamber with hazmat suits hanging on the sidewalls. On the other end of the chamber is a door that is completely sealed off from the rest of the world. Dr. Zazio casually explains the procedure of coming in to see this patient. "Elizabeth, it is very important that you do not go or come from this room freely. You will need mine or Dr. Holden's company while dealing with this one particular patient."

Elizabeth looks around and then looks through the second door's window. Elizabeth sees a short, bald man sitting naked on his bed. Neither the bed nor the room appear at all comfortable. The little man, named Danica Cyrus, doesn't look happy, just slightly irritated and bored.

Dr. Zazio looks down at Elizabeth, "Well you know what? It's most likely better if the original nurses deal with this patient, Mr. Cyrus. You see he has very severe allergies. He is allergic to almost everything."

"Why, yes of course. Cyrus, you say?" Elizabeth shakes her head in agreement.

She looks up to Dr. Zazio and he states, "Yes, Danica Cyrus. That's why he has to be in there…locked away."

"How does something like this even happen?"

"You know, it's the brain's ability to fight off infection. Or, I should say, his brain doesn't give his body what it needs to fight off the common complications of having allergies." Dr. Zazio begins to make his way out of the incubation chamber. Elizabeth follows, then stops and looks back again.

Danica rolls back on his bed with a heavy breath. Dr. Zazio steps out and continues, "But he is a tough one and he is very different…one of the staff members laughs about how he wasn't meant to be here on this planet that he was born to the wrong one."

Dr. Zazio lets out a small chuckle. Elizabeth walks out and looks back over the solid door while Dr. Zazio seals it closed.

Elizabeth feels bad for leaving a human being in such an enclosed area, even for his own good. They begin down the hallway, and Elizabeth gets a last look at the flashing red keypad on the outside of the wall.

Dr. Zazio walks toward the darkroom at the end of the hall. It has a creepy, dark vibe, and Elizabeth can feel it in her bones. Dr. Zazio points out the room, but before he gets to the empty darkness at the end of the hall, he has to make one more stop. He must introduce Elizabeth to the third and final patient in the main hall.

Dr. Zazio stops and grabs the door handle. This door is normal, and not only a typical door; the door is actually already propped open by its latch. Dr. Zazio pulls the already cracked open door the rest of the way open. Elizabeth walks up behind him in awe at what she sees.

Dr. Zazio walks into the room and makes himself known. "How are we today?" Dr. Zazio smiles and brings in Elizabeth. Dr. Zazio nods to Miss Walleton, sitting in the middle of the room with the patient.

Dr. Zazio introduces Elizabeth. "This is Miss Walleton, whom you know, and this is Mr. Linwood. How are you today Mr. Linwood?" Miss Walleton waves hi to Elizabeth and turns to her patient.

"Also known as Kyrose. Kyrose Linwood." Elizabeth is a little overwhelmed but is experienced and has already seen her share of off-the-wall things.

"Nice to meet you, Mr. Linwood. Can you speak?"

Dr. Zazio cuts in. "Not quite, not at this moment. As you can clearly see he has elephantiasis. It is severe on his right arm, up the left side of his head, and the top of his lap. It is also clearly in his left leg."

Dr. Zazio smiles at Kyrose and continues, "But that's not the reason he can't speak." Kyrose simply nods in agreement with the doctor. Dr. Zazio begins to make his way out of the room.

"Sorry to bother your session, Miss Walleton. Kyrose, thank you for your time. I was simply showing the new set of hands around." They walk to the exit and out the door.

Elizabeth smiles at them and then follows Dr. Zazio out. She is a curious one, or maybe simply just wants to know, so she asks, "Why can't he speak?" They continue down the hall toward the darkroom at the end. Dr. Zazio walks with his hands once again propped behind him.

"Well, the brain, Elizabeth. It's an amazing thing. One of my main studies on Kyrose is when the sickness entered a part of his brain." Dr. Zazio continues,

"You see, it changed him. In not only the physical way you can clearly see, but in a mental way also. I'm not positive just yet what happened, or how, but Kyrose can switch off parts of his body anywhere from not being able to speak, to not hydrating or eating for days at a time. Sometimes he doesn't eat for days and he's fine." Elizabeth follows, trying to keep up.

Dr. Zazio continues, "Some days he goes without water or food. Yet his vitals are normal and actually healthy."

"He can alter his life patterns?"

"Yes, and then some." They get to the last door and it's swung open already, and the pitch-black inside is astonishing. Elizabeth feels a cold presence in this last room. A camera sits at the top of the door, staring straight down at Elizabeth and down behind her at the rest of the hall.

Elizabeth sees the camera and then turns and looks back down the hallway, and another camera is set up at the other end, also above the stairs. Dr. Zazio stops and grins a little, then throws his jacket aside and pulls out a walkie-talkie.

He squeezes the trigger. "Simon copy…? Simon? We need the lights in Mr. Garner's room turned on, over."

Dr. Zazio waits for a second for any form of response. He squeezes it again, "Copy…?" Dr. Zazio waits, then looks into the camera's lens. Then, out of nowhere, the last room lights up.

Simon's voice replies back over the radio, scratchy, "Sorry."

The door is wide open and Dr. Zazio walks into the now-lit room. "This will be Bruce's room for his stay until we can heal him and get him to sleep."

Elizabeth's a little uneasy; the room is extra bright only because it's a pearl white padded room. The door is also padded. Elizabeth almost wants to cry. Dr. Zazio says, "Yes, yes. Bruce, he who cannot sleep. I think this is for his best."

Dr. Zazio walks over to the padded wall and unclicks a flatbed frame that folds down from the wall. He lowers it, then puts it back up. Elizabeth shakes it off and agrees with the doctor. She shakes her head casually, looking around.

Dr. Zazio watches her and realizes she won't make eye contact with him. Dr. Zazio looks around, understanding. "It's the sixth day he has been awake. He will soon lose his self-control. I know this seems like a bit much, but rest assured that everything's ready to go to treat him. That, and he is almost here."

***

The typical, white, panel van, with two tinted windows up front, pulls away from the previous hospital. They loaded

Bruce up, and now they're on their way. The van's tires catch grip, and they peel away on down the road. The driver sits up front alone.

He gets into traffic and then stops at the first stoplight. He looks back to the three riding in the back and then makes the necessary left and gasses out onto the freeway. They are heading toward Dr. Zazio's Hospital Necropolis. The driver moves the van along, swiftly.

The three men in the back of the van haven't really said much. There are two nurses and the patient, Bruce Garner. Bruce sits in the very back of the van. He sits up against the sidewall.

They have him wearing a straightjacket. It's for the transfer, so he doesn't lash out or hurt himself the results of being unstable. The driver looks back at him; he watches him through the rearview mirror. Bruce turns and makes complete eye contact with him.

Bruce is loopy, and his appearance is disturbing and off-putting. The driver merges into another lane of traffic, speeding along the way. Bruce sits and stares at the rearview mirror. The driver looks back, uncomfortable, and flicks the rearview mirror up and out of view.

He shakes off Bruce's vibe while trying to concentrate on the road. Bruce is clearly wearing a different vibe all over his persona. It's an intense vibe attached to him, a complete one-eighty from when he first showed up at the hospital. Brett is one of the two male nurses in the back of the van.

The other nurse is Jasper. He's only along for the ride for the transfer. He's a slightly built man, and he sits the closest to Bruce, holding onto him as the driver proceeds off of the highway. Bruce sits up against the back of the van then, throws a leg up on the seat in front of him.

Brett looks over his leg and then up at Bruce. Bruce sits there in his jacket not saying a word or moving. He only wears a creepy smile with wide eyes. Brett is speechless but watches Bruce.

Bruce is not really blinking. Brett gulps while Bruce stares, silent. A small grunt from Bruce and Brett squirms and jumps a little. The other nurse laughs at Brett and then looks to Bruce. Bruce slowly directs his attention to Jasper.

Bruce makes eye contact then forces out a loud, creepy laugh. The laugh drops Jasper's stomach while Bruce makes complete eye contact with him. Brett gets uneasy while Bruce turns back and laughs again, this time a little louder. This has Brett almost in tears with simple fear.

The driver grabs his rearview mirror, adjusting it to the back. He instantly regrets it when he makes eye contact with the smiling Bruce. The driver drops the rearview mirror and speeds up. Then, just like that, Bruce switches; he becomes completely normal and the smile's gone.

He seems more calm and human just like that, out of nowhere. He looks around him, slightly confused, and then puts his leg down and sits upright with complete balance. This catches both of the nurses off guard. The van is getting close to the hospital.

Hopefully, it's the place where Bruce will finally get help. Bruce is silent then turns to Jasper, sitting next to him. Bruce tries to talk to him, "So…what do you think happens to you when you sleep?"

Jasper gets a little on guard and responds, "Sir, if you just relax, we will be at the hospital in a minute."

Jasper tries to comfort Bruce in a sense while avoiding his gibberish.

Bruce continues, "Well. I will have you know, I'm from a very different existence." Bruce turns and smiles at Brett and continues, "When you sleep, you wash away the entity that consumes the body on that day."

The two nurses look at each other in confusion. Bruce's shoulders arch back and his eyes roll into the back of his head.

Brett jumps up in the van and with fear in his voice shouts, "What is he doing?" Bruce starts to shake and space out.

His actions scare Brett beyond words. Jasper screams out, "He's having a seizure!" The driver hears him loud and clear and reaches over to the passenger seat. He grabs a portable siren and then rolls the window down just enough to force his arm out and slam the siren down on the roof of the van.

The van picks up speed down the road. Brett takes a deep breath. "We need to lay him down." The other nurse grabs his legs.

Brett grabs Bruce's torso and they adjust him to lie down in the back of the van. Bruce shakes violently a little more, then he freezes up. Silence. They look Bruce over and then out of nowhere, he lets out what could only be described as a howl.

Both nurses jump back. Bruce stops and is once again silent. Brett leans back and awkwardly says to the driver, "I don't know what the hell that was, but get us there already." Brett turns and looks at Jasper then they both turn to Bruce.

Bruce lies still, then slowly his head rolls over to the left. He looks directly at the two of them wearing the once-again enormous smile. Bruce opens his mouth and, with a deep, creepy voice, says. "You only get one day to be in the human body. That's why suicide is so bad!"

Bruce quickly sits up with a twitch and continues, "Suicide would be based on one entity's choice to kill that masterpiece of the body. I love this one…and I never want to leave."

***

Elizabeth rushes out of the building; she has been speed walking ever since she heard Simon's voice over Dr. Zazio's radio. She heard, "Bruce's transportation has just pulled up." Elizabeth exits the tiny building with Dr. Zazio on her tail. Simon holds the door open for the two of them.

Simon then goes back inside and watches the security cameras. Elizabeth walks out and looks high into the air, happy to feel the light on her face. She wasn't down there for too long, but it still felt like forever. The white van with no side windows sits at the gate, stopped.

It's stopped, but the red light still flashes on the rooftop. Dr. Zazio turns around and walks back to the building. He opens the door to the hospital and looks inside at Simon sitting watching the monitors. "Open the gate for them. What are you doing?"

Simon reaches over and turns a key then hits a red button. Dr. Zazio, still with his head peeked in, yells, "Serana!" He waits, and sure enough, she comes running up from the bottom level. Serana comes around the lounge and sees Dr. Zazio's head peeking in.

Dr. Zazio adjusts the open door and stands upright. "Go get Mr. Garner's room finished and ready. He is here." Serana nods and rushes back into the lounge and then down to the hospital.

Elizabeth sees the gate slide open and the van pulls in. She feels a strange vibe as the van is pulling up to the hospital. Elizabeth looks back to Dr. Zazio and says nervously, "Didn't you say there were two doctors?"

"Yes."

"Yourself and…"

She gets cut off by Dr. Zazio, "Holden. Yes, he will be here in a few hours. After we get Bruce settled in." The van comes to a screeching halt in front of them.

The driver hops out of the van quickly and in some sort of panic. The driver rushes to the back of the van and then waves Dr. Zazio and Elizabeth over. "We had some problems." They rush up to the back door, but before they can touch it.

It, swings open in a panic. Jasper bolts out of the back of the van. His face is pale, emotionless, and dropped; he looks like he wants to throw-up. He pushes past Elizabeth and Dr. Zazio.

They are both quick to look inside the van. Elizabeth is taken back at what she sees. Bruce is sitting up straight, looking at them with a terrible smile. Brett stands in the back of the van, just staring at Bruce.

Brett is clearly wearing a form of fear and confusion smeared across his face. Dr. Zazio watches as Brett is in a panic. Dr. Zazio calls out, "What happened in here…? Brett?"

Brett looks over, then shakes it off and slowly goes to help get Bruce out of the van. Dr. Zazio and Elizabeth begin to help him. They slide Bruce down the seat. Dr. Zazio waves over to Simon, implying for him to come out.

Brett stops, gets out of the van, and walks away in a form of confusion. Elizabeth's jaw is dropped over his actions. Dr. Zazio is concerned as Brett slowly walks away. He calls out, "Brett."

Elizabeth and Dr. Zazio look back to Bruce sitting in the van, smiling.

Chapter 8
May 23ʳᵈ, 1998 (JASPER)

Elizabeth breathes heavily, looking into the mirror, standing once again in the women's restroom at the courthouse. She keeps eye contact with herself, then steps back and leans on the sink. She puts her head down and lets out a deep sigh, feeling a little nauseous. She knows she only feels this way because she's still extremely confused over what is actually happening, or for that matter, what has happened.

Elizabeth lets out another deep sigh and looks at herself in the mirror once again. She puts her hands lightly on the skin of her pale face and, with a quiet voice, tells herself, "I don't even know who you are." Elizabeth is quickly interrupted by an older woman; making her way into the restroom. The woman shoves open the door and walks past Elizabeth.

Elizabeth casually turns on the water faucet, finishing her routine in the bathroom. Another thought grabs her attention while she looks down, letting the water run across her hands and through her fingers. She feels frightened to have these memories, these thoughts. She feels lost confused about who or even what she is.

Now the confusion arises over what the human body really is. Elizabeth stares at the water running…*bang*. The stall door closes behind the woman and then the toilet seat drops. The noise snaps Elizabeth back into her reality once again.

Elizabeth feels like she's falling apart, but she knows she needs to keep it together. She dries her hands off and grabs her bag but stops in mid-strut. She's about to go back to the courtroom, but she wants and needs to look into the mirror one last time. She needs to look, not to see her body or her face, but to make eye contact with herself.

She wants to make sure she knows the woman that is in the mirror. Elizabeth turns slightly and looks at the mirror, and all she does is confuse herself even more. With a sigh, she looks down and walks out of the bathroom, still drying her hands and staring at the tile floor as she walks. Elizabeth is in deep thought, but it's quickly cut off by the sound of a couple coming from around the corner.

She is instantly cut off by her mother and Tamara. She drops her defense and actually smiles. "Mom." Her mom is older but still moves unnaturally fast to give her daughter a tight hug. Tamara rubs Elizabeth's arm, and then Elizabeth lets go of her mom and gives Tamara a hug as well.

Tears already stream down Elizabeth's face. It's clear, she's in some sort of turmoil and confusion. Elizabeth's mom looks her over. "Are you okay with this?"

Elizabeth smiles and replies, "Yeah, I think everyone needs to know the details of all of this, all that's happened." Tamara is a true friend, showing any form of reassurance.

"You got this. You're not the one in the wrong here. I don't know if it feels like it, but we are all here for you."

Elizabeth has to give her another hug. "Thank you, Tamara." Elizabeth looks at them and continues. "I couldn't do this, relive any of this without your guys' support."

Elizabeth looks at Tamara then around. "Where's Jordan?" Tamara throws a shrug.

"He was still sitting in the courtroom when we got up to come find you."

Tamara stops talking when she feels the presence of someone behind her. Mr. Garner walks up to the three of them. Elizabeth stops with a sigh of relief when she sees Mr. Garner walk up to her with his arms out for a hug. His nurse walks calmly behind him.

He gives Elizabeth the best sigh of relief. He lets go and looks at her as a tear rolls out of her already puffy eyes. "So, you're my boy's honeybunch? Good choice, good choice."

He smiles and then gives her another tight hug. He stops and then turns around to the nurse. He begins to pat himself down. "He wanted to meet you," the nurse tells Elizabeth.

Mr. Garner makes grieving eye contact with Elizabeth, then walks away with the nurse leading him back to his seat.

The stand is empty in the courtroom, and the noise level has risen on the account of being in recess. The senseless bickering and chatting gets put to a halt by the judge's mallet. He slams it down with a clear signal that they are about to begin. It's once again silent.

Wilson takes the stage; he walks up to the middle of the courtroom floor in front of the judge to announce another witness to the stand.

Wilson, with a stern, attention grabbing voice, begins, "Before we start this next session of events…" Wilson walks around, smiling at the prosecutor.

"I would like to call, Jasper Hanney to the stand, the second nurse that was in the van that early morning. I want to call him up to verify *my* client, Ms. Primrose's story."

The judge nods, and Wilson says again with a raised voice, "I would like to call, Mr. Hanney to the stand." The entire courtroom turns around as the doors get pushed open by two guards.

Mr. Hanney makes his way to the front of the courtroom. Jasper tries to hold his head high. He's nervous, but who wouldn't be, having to give your statement to an entire courtroom. Jasper walks down and swings open the small gate, and then with a deep breath, looking over the stand.

Jasper looks up to the judge and walks past Wilson, up to the officer that is going to swear him in. He looks over the courtroom after swearing-in.

Jasper still trying to get comfortable in the chair, as Wilson strutting up with a smile. The door swings open in the back of the room and hit the officer that is standing tall. Elizabeth is trying her hardest to be quiet, but in some way, it all turns wrong. Already once again, she is the center of attention. The crowd turns and it's clear she's been noticed and quietly judged in every way.

Simultaneously, they all turn back around. The guard moves and opens the door the rest of the way for her. Elizabeth tries to act calm, but she is pale and clearly, shaken. She walks down and back to the front of the courtroom and sits at the vacant table on the left.

The defense attorney is in the middle of his questioning with Mr. Hanney. Wilson paces, trying to be precise in his questions. "So, you would say he was acting in an odd and off-putting manner? Was Bruce acting this way because of no sleep?"

She watches Jasper's reaction to the situation. "Oh, most definitely."

"Was he at all violent?"

"No. I would say that he was more lost, but it's what he had said that threw me off. That wasn't a human talking. Well, let's just say, if anything, it was the third person; it wasn't at all natural."

Mr. Hanney's eyes get large, then wander to the floor. He's clearly a scared and confused man over all this.

Wilson nods and faces the judge with confidence. "I rest my case."

The judge sits up and clears his throat. "Council, do you have anything to ask this young man?"

The prosecutor sits tightly in his seat and then stands. "Yes, your honor."

He stands up and walks out to the floor and takes control. "Was *he*, and by *he,* I mean, Bruce Garner, on any kind of medication at this point?"

Mr. Hanney answers with pure honesty, "Not that I know. All I can prove is what it said in the report. It said, 'His body was for some unexplained reason flushing every medication given to help him straight out of his body.' But as far as I was concerned, he was clean."

The prosecutor nods to the jury and to the judge. "No more questions."

The prosecutor sits back down. The judge sits up and looks over some papers and nods to the guard to remove Mr. Hanney from the stand.

The judge looks back down at Elizabeth. "Are you ready to continue?"

Elizabeth nods yes to the judge. The judge is not having it.

"Speak up, ma'am!"

Elizabeth gets a loose tongue really quick. "Yes sir, I am."

The judge puts his hand out, implying for her to come back up to the stand. "Well, alright then." Elizabeth is once again sworn in, and the prosecutor gets back to his feet. Elizabeth tries to get comfortable well as comfortable as she can. Elizabeth tries to catch her breath to at least be able to speak.

The prosecutor walks in a pacing manner, "Ms. Primrose you were there when Bruce Garner had just arrived at Dr. Zazio's hospital. So…if you would like to take it from there."

Elizabeth looks over the crowd that is sitting, anxiously waiting for her to continue. Elizabeth tries to speak clearly, "Yes, he showed up, and the two nurses jumped out of the back of the van."

Elizabeth's voice gets shaky. "Then, we put Bruce in his room. We were all very quick to close the door on him." Elizabeth tears up and grabs a tissue. She takes a deep breath, fights back the tears, and tries to calm down and continue.

"Bruce was in his room sitting quietly. He had to be sad. Sad that no one wanted to be near him…not even me."

The prosecutor leans back on his table, listening closely to Elizabeth but questioning her words. "He was alone? And where was his family, his parents, at this time?"

Elizabeth stops and thinks out loud. "Well this was the sixth day he had been awake, but we only found out on the fourth day that he couldn't sleep. You must understand that something like this happens fast. I'm not positive where they were."

"But they were contacted?"

"Well, I was told that Dr. Blankly had first contacted them, but that was on the fourth day. I'm not positive if he ever got ahold of anyone."

"Did *you* ever try calling them? A family member?"

"I did actually; it was later that day after Bruce was dropped off at Hospital Necropolis. I was disgusted with myself for not wanting to be near him, but he was so cynical and the vibe that was there…I couldn't. But I knew someone needed to be there." Elizabeth looks at Mr. Garner sitting in the crowd with his nurse.

He sits and stares silently. She smiles at him, then shakes it off and continues. "I had to leave, so I left Hospital Necropolis. I had to get my thoughts together."

The prosecutor gets even more comfortable leaning up against his table.

"Continue."

Chapter 9
May 13th, 1998 – 7:15 P.M.
(Dr. Holden)

Elizabeth drives fast down the freeway with her windows down and the cool wind running through her hair. She's letting it hit her face as she rushes away from the hospital feeling the freedom of being able to run away and actually doing it. Her foot gains weight on the gas pedal, not sure where she's going, but wanting to get there fast. Her car takes another left, deeper into the middle of nowhere, far from everything.

The gas pedal of her car hits the floor. Elizabeth turns up the music to a great song, and it makes her feel free from all the bad energy. The engine revs loud and strong. Then Elizabeth lets loose and calms back down with a deep sigh of pure confusion.

She takes another left down a long lonely road. She slows and looks to the skies in the west, watching the sunset. It shines brightly into her eyes as she flies by, trying her hardest to free her mind again. The sun is welcoming, and it feels like it can help her for that moment.

Elizabeth watches the sun slowly get eaten up as the clouds roll in. And just like that the sun is gone, covered up. Dark clouds roll in with a strike of lightning in the distance. Elizabeth lets off the pedal and takes the next turn back into town, an exit far away from everything.

She turns her back on the storm heading her way.

***

Elizabeth's car is parked in the corner of a vacant convenient store parking lot. The rain has begun to come down, harder and harder with every second. Elizabeth's in a panic and runs from the store to her car. A *beep* and the car flashes, its lights are on; unlocked. Elizabeth swings open the driver's side door and then flings her snacks into the car's passenger seat. She jumps in the driver's seat and swings the door closed in a panic from the rain. She sets her drink in the console next to her.

Then puts her hands on the steering wheel, and hangs her head. Waves of confusion. Her own thoughts are tearing her down like waves on the beach. Gone for a second, but destined to return destroying her in her never-ending reality.

Elizabeth throws her head back, fed-up with this fight. A clap of thunder crashes. It gets the entire world's attention. The clap of thunder seems to open up the sky, making it rain even harder.

The sky has Elizabeth's complete attention. It pours rain harder and harder. She looks over to her snacks in the passenger seat and her drink on the console. Avoids all thoughts and grabs her drink.

She decided on coffee. The right drink for the rain. Elizabeth sips, and watches the rain hit the hood of her car. She looks over her clothes; soaked from the short run.

She cleans the water off the door panel, and looks over and wipes off the interior of her car. She stops and takes another sip of her coffee, ever so softly. Then she looks to the bag of snacks next to her and decides to go through it. She grabs a snack bar.

She rips open the wrapper and takes a monster bite. She puts her head on the window looking out to the rain. A flash of lightning strikes. Unfortunately for Elizabeth, along with the flash is the thought of what to do about Bruce.

It is like feeling an instant case of anxiety. Elizabeth looks over her chocolate bar and, with an enormous sense of self-pity, breaks down and cries. Elizabeth wants these thoughts blocked out. Blocked out if only for another second.

Elizabeth puts down her candy bar and begins searching for her keys. She then puts her coffee down and still continues searching. Elizabeth finds her keys under her thigh from panicking and jumping in the vehicle. She pulls them out and starts the car for the relief of the radio.

The engine turns over and the radio kicks on. It's a slow song playing. Elizabeth turns it down. She looks over to her snacks and picks them back up.

She sees her phone. It sits in the passenger seat. Elizabeth grabs it and turns it on. She needs someone to help her through this situation.

She knows she needs any form of guidance. Who can she get good information from, it's something she feels is the hardest thing to find. In realization maybe there is no help, maybe she needs to be tough. Maybe she needs to be at the hospital with hands-on

Elizabeth knows Bruce needs someone. She begins to wonder, where Bruce's family is. She needs to find them, but she's not sure where to begin. They weren't together long enough for Elizabeth to meet them, much less get contact information.

Elizabeth puts her phone down in defeat but then remembers Bruce using her phone a few weeks back. He needed to use it to call his dad! She moves quickly and actually finds what she thinks is the number he dialed. She has to at least try.

Bruce needs someone he knows next to him. The phone rings loud, for the third time. Elizabeth listens but is in a slight shock at who answers. "Saint Cliff, Nursing Home."

Elizabeth is almost speechless. The caller on the other line is confused as well, and you can hear it in his voice as Elizabeth hangs up the phone. Elizabeth caught off guard. Then she acts again and calls Dr. Blankly.

The phone goes straight to his voice mail. Elizabeth fed up, feeling helpless. She throws her phone down on the seat next to her; in a fit of rage. The rain pours and for some reason ceases to stop.

It looks like it's here to stay as another lightning strike, crashes and shakes the car. Elizabeth grabs the gearshift and throws it in to drive. She squeals the tires and gets on the road. She grabs her coffee, not in too much of a hurry to get back to that awkward situation.

She has to be there, and she knows it's going to be one of the hardest things she might ever have to do, but she knows Bruce needs her.

Elizabeth runs up to the front entrance of Hospital Necropolis. She hopes the door to this place would be open, but it's not. Elizabeth in a panic leaps up and down in front of the camera. The rain pours hard, small puddles accumulating all around her as the result.

Elizabeth in a panic gets soaked, but finally, a sigh of relief when she hears the door click open. She quickly swings open the door and runs inside. Simon closes the door behind her. She shakes off the rain.

Simon stands tall with a towel, in hand. He hands it over quickly and with an apology. "Sorry, I ran downstairs." Simon walks to the second door and pulls it open.

"After you." Simon holds the door open. Elizabeth smiles at the gentle giant and walks through the second door. Simon follows behind her; she walks past his station and toward the breakroom.

Simon goes into his station and goes to work. Elizabeth walks into the break room, interrupted with the strong smell of coffee. It's being poured. A stream of coffee pours into a glass mug.

It's held by Dr. Holden; the second doctor at the facility. Elizabeth walks in and interrupts him with her presence. Dr. Holden stops pouring his coffee, smiles, and addresses Elizabeth. "Ah, you must be Elizabeth?"

He puts down the pot of coffee and throws his lab coat aside. He's confident and full of charisma. He grabs a spoon for the sugar and begins to mix his coffee. Elizabeth has a sigh of relief when she sees him.

Elizabeth smiles, "Yes of course. You must be Dr. Holden?" He puts his cup on the counter and walks over to Elizabeth with a smile and his hand out. Elizabeth has a smile spread across her face; she feels a warm calming vibe from him.

She looks him over, shakes his hand and comments. "It's nice to finally meet you."

"Same here. I have also had the chance to finally meet Mr. Garner as well. And I must tell you, I'm on my game to get him to go to sleep. I've already had a great opportunity to look over his sleep patterns and his circadian. I'm going to give it my best."

He stops talking, and Dr. Holden can clearly see that bringing this subject up is hard on her. But Holden also knows it has to be brought up and faced. "I know, it's hard but we don't have much time. Especially how Bruce is changing and handling all of this. I mean he's been awake for already six days and in nine hours it will be seven."

Holden walks back to his cup of coffee and continues. "I will be here working all night. I need to find out how we can get him back to sleep, and why he's rejecting what medicine we do give him." Elizabeth with a sigh of relief feels a lot better about the situation.

So much that she almost can't show her full gratitude. "Thank you for trying for him. I'm worried, but I will try my best to help. I do want to be here."

Holden smiles once again, then turns away. Elizabeth returns the smile, but there is something that catches her eye as he turns. His lab coat catches air and Elizabeth has a clear view of a handgun holstered on his pants. Dr. Holden continues the conversation with the assumption that nothing had changed.

"That's good to know. It's good to have an extra hand in the hospital."

Elizabeth is slightly concerned, "Dr. Holden? Why are you carrying a weapon? Why do we need so many guns in here?"

Holden caught off guard and looks down at his side. He pulls his lab coat back over his holster and turns to Elizabeth. "Does it bother you? No need to worry. I guess I didn't introduce myself properly. I'm also an officer and licensed."

Elizabeth agrees and shakes it off. Dr. Holden continues, "It's only for safety. You see some of the patients in this hospital at some point are and have been felons. Unfortunately for Dr. Zazio and myself, we specialize in special illnesses that require being around the mentally ill. But I promise this thing has never come out of its holster while I've had it. That's eight years, in this hospital. So, no worries."

Once again, he gives her a smile, and deep down she believes him. He takes a sip of his coffee and makes a displeased face. Dr. Holden walks back over and puts a few more spoonful of sugar in it. He continues to stir his coffee.

"You know, I have a few ideas on how to get Bruce back to sleep…" Holden gets cut off by Dr. Zazio walking around the corner, coming up from the lower part of the hospital. Dr. Zazio walks up and casually smiles at Dr. Holden. Then he sees Elizabeth.

"Elizabeth, you're here? I was wondering where you had run off to." Elizabeth still wipes the rain from her hair and clothes.

"Yeah, I needed a minute to breathe."

Dr. Zazio smiles at her, and Elizabeth looks down while saying, "I was trying to get a hold of any of Bruce's relatives, but I didn't have any luck. Have you talked with any of his relatives?"

"Not yet, I thought Dr. Blankly was already handling those arrangements. But I will look into it." Dr. Zazio finishes with a nod to Elizabeth and he continues.

"Yes, and are you going to go down and meet with Bruce? I left Brett down there with him, but you can go down and takeover his shift watching over him. If you like."

Elizabeth instantly looks down and away. She has to get up the nerve to go down there. She hasn't really sat and talked with Bruce, while he's in this mind state. Deep down Elizabeth doesn't really know if she can.

Lightning strikes and it's followed by a clap of thunder. The thunder catches all their attention, instantly. Elizabeth takes off her wet jacket and throws it on the chair next to her. "Well, I think I should go see if he needs anything."

Miss Walleton comes around the corner into the break room and smiles at Elizabeth. Elizabeth nervously walks toward the lower part of the hospital. She gets interrupted as she walks past Dr. Holden. Dr. Holden can see Elizabeth shaken, clearly nervous.

He watches and comments, "If you need anything at all, just call. Actually, you know what, I'll walk you down there." Holden's voice sits calmly in her ear. She turns and smiles with a face full of grief and thankfulness.

Dr. Holden holds his coffee tight, follows Elizabeth. They both head down.

Dr. Holden and Elizabeth both feel a slight drop in temperature, while they go down these concrete stairs. They reach the bottom side by side; it takes a minute for their eyes to dilate and adjust. Elizabeth looks down the long hallway; all the way to the end. She gets a slight chill.

A chill that runs deep up her spine. Elizabeth with a loss of air looks over to Dr. Holden. He can see it in her eyes, fear. She almost wants to call it quits and turn around.

Elizabeth knows deep down, if she does that, it wouldn't stop there. She would also run straight out of the hospital. Dr. Holden walks next to her, they continue, "I need to be in the laboratory. I think this is where I leave y…"

Elizabeth cuts him off, by stopping in mid-stride, and then pulls away and turns around. "I don't know if I can do this. He is so far gone; I'm terrified of this." Dr. Holden feels her stress as it comes on strong, but he tries his best to calm her.

"Look, I know somewhat of the kind of person that you are. I can also see what this man means to you. And if those feelings are real, I think maybe he needs you as much as you need him." Elizabeth stumbles back and leans up against the wall.

It's clear she's hesitant and purposely delaying. She gets her thoughts cut off by Bruce's door. It opens in the distance. Brett comes out and closes the door behind him.

Brett walks out traumatize. He wears a look like he just witnessed something terrible happen. He walks out slowly then lifts his head up and sees Dr. Holden and Elizabeth standing at the end of the hallway. It puts a slight smile on his face.

He is happy to see two other colleagues. Brett picks up his pace and walks up to the two of them. Brett stops then goes to Elizabeth with his arms out, "I'm sorry, come here. Bring it in."

Brett stretches his arms out for a hug. Elizabeth goes in and gets a tight hug. She looks at the door in the distance over Brett's shoulder. Brett squeezes tight and then let's go.

They all three make their way toward the end of the hallway. Dr. Holden and Brett stop and wave her on. They talk to each other while Elizabeth walks toward Bruce's room. They watch her.

Elizabeth keeps walking and their conversation, because of the distance becomes simple gibberish. The one thing, Elizabeth makes out from their conversation right when she gets to Bruce's door is, "Too far gone." Elizabeth freezes still and takes a deep breath, their gibberish continues.

She turns around and they both smile and proceed in their separate directions. Brett runs toward the stairs leading to the lounge. Dr. Holden makes a left into the laboratory. Elizabeth turns back around standing in front of Bruce's door.

She takes a deep breath and looks inside the door's window. Bruce paces back and forth in this soft, padded room. He simply paces, it looks like he is talking to himself. She watches him for a second then he stops.

With a twitch. He turns and looks at her through the glass window. She takes a breath and looks away, down to the handle of the door. She proceeds to open the door.

She then looks back up and Bruce is in the window, looking straight at her. She stops and gets wide-eyed. He quickly backs up into the middle of the room. Elizabeth opens the door with what is the best attempt of confidence that she has in her. "Bruce, you scared me."

Bruce steps back in a gentleman type of way. He waves his hand for her to enter the room while he bows. He takes a few more steps back, holds his bow. Elizabeth tries to hold her composer and walk in. "Bruce, stop being that way. We need to talk, please sit down."

He looks at her and smiles. His eyes are bloodshot red. He has lost a lot of weight; around fifty pounds. He is a lot skinnier than Elizabeth has ever seen him.

He smiles and lets his shoulders drop down and then sits on his bed. Bruce sits still and in his regular voice, "Alright. Let's talk." Elizabeth caught off guard because he appears himself for the moment.

It's almost a relief to know Bruce is in there. Elizabeth steps further in the room and continues. "Bruce, first I need to talk about the situation that we are in. I know I need to be professional, but I need something from you also. I need you to try and sleep for me. I know you tried, but…Bruce."

Bruce turns to her and shakes his head. "Sleep?"

"Yes honey, we need you to try and sleep."

Bruce continues on, "I'm trying, I can't do it. I've been counting the minutes, the hours and now days. I can't…sleep."

Elizabeth feels a sense of calm and understanding coming from Bruce. She comes into the room a little further. She keeps her eyes on him sitting on the bed. He has his head down, talking.

She feels comfortable enough to get closer to him. Elizabeth keeps her composer and sits down next to him on the bed, and continues. "The doctors here are trying to help you, and I'm trying to help you. We need you to be strong."

Bruce keeps his head down and replies, in the simplest tone. "I'm trying. I'm just counting, I can't sleep so I count. I count when I'm alone, and I count when I'm not me…I count." Elizabeth is quick to respond and talk with him.

"Not you?"

Bruce looks at her with a tear in his eye, "I feel it in me. Ever since I woke it…it becomes me." Elizabeth can feel his pain, it tears her up inside, not knowing what to do.

"Bruce, we don't know how staying awake for so long will even affect you. Not to mention your wound. A lot of it will be in your head."

"It's a part of us, I can feel it. I'm losing this fight." Bruce replies then reach over and touches Elizabeth's leg. It's such a familiar thing.

She puts her hand on top of his. Yet a simple movement, but can change your mood instantly. This catches Elizabeth off guard, she notices Bruce's fingers. They're chewed up with eminence of blood covering the tips.

Bruce turns to hide the tears and the pure confusion coming from him. Elizabeth tries to console him and give him the strength of any sort.

Confused, Elizabeth is terrified for Bruce, but she keeps encouraging. "The doctors and staff here are good people, they are."

Bruce still sits with his hand on her leg and with his head turned away. He's silent…then.

"I've been counting, the minutes, hours, and now days. I can't sleep."

"We have a few ideas…"

"I'm trying. I'm just counting, but I can't sleep, so I count. I count when I'm alone, and I count when I'm not me…I count."

"Bruce, I think you…"

"I've been counting the minutes, hours, and now days. I can't sleep."

"Bruce are you…"

"I'm trying. I'm just counting, I can't sleep so I count. I count when I'm alone, and I count when I'm not me…I count." Bruce continues to repeat himself then his grasp on Elizabeth's leg grows tighter. Her heart picks up pace.

It's an instant fear creeping over her. Bruce still sits, looking away. "I'm trying. I'm just counting, I can't sleep. So, I count."

He turns back to her with a creepy smile. Then his eyes roll into the back of his head, and he shakes violently! Elizabeth pulls away and stands up in a slight shock. "Bruce! Bruce?"

Elizabeth not sure what to do. She thinks it might be a seizure. "Bruce?" He stops shaking then lies down, and grins a nasty smile.

He locks eyes with Elizabeth and begins to talk gibberish. She can't make any of it out. Elizabeth backs up toward the door and stares at him. He begins shouting and screaming.

Elizabeth is paralyzed by fear. Bruce stops and smiles. Elizabeth watches him switch; frozen in fear she stares at him, speechless. She can't take it and forces herself to turn away.

Then one thing gets her attention. She's not sure how she should feel about it. She turns toward Bruce terrified simply because of what she has seen in the corner of the room. A straightjacket lies up against the wall in the back.

She clearly remembers Bruce wearing one when he arrived. She turns back around toward the door in confusion, hoping that Brett had taken the jacket off of him. She turns and faces Bruce.

It's like night and day.

He sits up and has the most disturbing face. It is as if it's not even him anymore. Elizabeth's heart thumps loud, then the smile on Bruce becomes wider.

He drools and begins to speak. "I'm so happy for everyone who is awake in life, not only awake but alive! A beautiful day, of pure energy. Then the next day you are tired, lazy, exhausted for no apparent reason. Why does the body change from day to day?"

Bruce smiles wider, stares unblinking at Elizabeth, and he continues. "Because of us. Of me and of others!" Elizabeth tries to understand him to some degree.

He drools even more through the smile. He stands up and takes a step toward Elizabeth. Bruce looks her in the eye, and with a deep unnatural voice. "You need to sleep to clean yourself from us."

Chapter 10
May 14ᵗʰ, 1998 (Want Sleep)

The courtroom watches on as Elizabeth gasps for air and quickly covers her mouth with her hand. The tension is thick, and silence has filled the courtroom from end to end. She looks over everyone including the prosecutor standing and listening avidly to Elizabeth's side of the story. Elizabeth has let her guard down a tad bit, but she is still trying to keep her composure.

She looks down at her palms and the waded-up tissue. "I tried my best to be calm and I walked out of the door." The prosecutor snaps back into action.

"Before you left, what went through your mind? How did his words really affect you? I believe the jury would like to feel closer to your view of the story." Elizabeth looks up from her hands and stares at him with a pinch of anger.

"How did it affect me? How would those words affect you? How would they affect any of you?" The jury and judge sit in silence over the thought of what Bruce had actually said.

Elizabeth calms and continues, "Bruce was a man that I got to know rather well over a few months. Now I don't know who I was talking to in that room, but that wasn't him." Elizabeth looks over the crowd and only feels crazy in their eyes, but the thoughts and actions are as real as can be.

Elizabeth takes a breath and continues, "You all need to know how importantly different this situation really is." The prosecutor seems emotionless as he shakes his head and walks back to his notes. Elizabeth feels lost, watching him.

She only hopes it's just a front to remain in character. He continues, "So you calmly walked out of his room? What did you do then?" The prosecutor looks her over and walks back toward the stand

"What happened after you left him?"

Once again, the eyes are all on Elizabeth awaiting any simple response. "I went and got one of the doctors, Dr. Zazio, I believe. I wasn't sure how to handle him by myself. I was terrified."

Wilson finally looks up from his notes and gives Elizabeth a nod and smile for simple support. Wilson stands up. "I think she needs a break."

The prosecutor looks back at Wilson, and with a coy smile, replies, "We will, we will. I just want to get this straight."

Elizabeth glares at the prosecutor and then looks to the jury before turning to the crowd that fills out all the seats. The prosecutor tries to get everything straight in his head. "Elizabeth, now you said he was moving around freely in this padded hospital room. Was his straightjacket removed or was he helped out of it?"

Elizabeth gets chills up her spine. "No, he wasn't helped out of it, and we still don't know how he got it off. Brett had also mentioned he was wearing it when he left the room, right before I walked in." The prosecutor walks back and forth.

"So, after this incident is when they put a camera up in his room?"

Elizabeth respectfully responds, "Yes, the next day."

"So now whoever's on guard can keep an eye on him or whoever is in that room?"

"Yes, they thought it would be best to monitor his every move."

Once again, the prosecutor puts his hands in his pockets and continues on his path for the truth. "So how long had Bruce been awake at this point?" Elizabeth thinks for a second, not wanting to get anyone confused.

"The mounting of the camera took place on the seventh day, that night. The next day was the eighth day, one hundred and ninety-two hours."

Knowing the exact time of how long Bruce had actually been awake caught even the prosecutor off guard. "So, it's going on the next day, day eight."

Elizabeth takes the reigns. "Yes, day eight. I actually got some sleep that night, and I was quickly at the hospital that morning."

***

The sun is rising bright in the sky, but it's pointless to even dream or think about it. It is too pointless to think about and is altogether heartbreaking. The amazing sunshine has been blocked out and held away from Elizabeth. Elizabeth is stuck down at the bottom of this hospital, trying to keep her sanity and her life together.

She is stuck down there with its dark cold concrete floor and the steel doors by her every passing side. A cold door handle gets turned to open one of the doors. The door unlatches and gets pushed open by Serana. Elizabeth's view into the room is blocked by Serana as she leads the way inside.

Elizabeth is following Serana around the hospital, with Miss Walleton following only a few steps behind. Serana pushes the door the rest of the way open and they all crowd into Kyrose's hospital room. Brett already sits with him, as they work together. Their space is instantly invaded when everyone piles in.

Brett and Kyrose look at each other with a surprised look on their faces. Miss Walleton storms in. "Sorry if we are being nosy or intruding. I thought we would try to show Elizabeth the ropes and the rest of the rules of Hospital Necropolis today."

Brett sits smiling with Kyrose. Kyrose has an awkward smile on his face, but it is a smile. Elizabeth stands between the other nurses staring enticingly at Kyrose. Elizabeth looks away.

She's curious, but she doesn't want to stare or be rude. Miss Walleton steps forward and, with a stern voice, addresses Brett. "How much longer do you have with Kyrose? Because you still need to go do the vitals on Mr. Garner in the back room."

Miss Walleton turns around, looking over Kyrose's room. Miss Walleton's presence always puts laughter or any form of happiness to a halt. Brett gets Kyrose's attention by hitting him on the leg. Then, Brett starts mimicking Miss Walleton behind her back by flapping his arms and head, with a complaining expression spread across his face.

Miss Walleton has always been the stern type at the hospital, but she is only taken about 70% seriously. Elizabeth and Nurse Serana chuckle, and Kyrose has an enormous smile on his face. Miss Walleton turns around and sees them all laughing at her expense. She just shakes her head disapprovingly.

Brett sits in deep thought for a bit, then gets flustered and frustrated. "I don't want to go in that room. No offense Elizabeth, but he terrifies me." Serana jumps in.

"Now don't be a little girl. You only need to take his vitals. He's only a patient. He hasn't even proven to be violent, just *majorly* unstable."

"Well if you think it's just that…then why don't you take his vitals?" Brett says with a cocky smile.

Miss Walleton is fed up with this pointless bickering and speaks up, "No. I said you. I need Serana for something else."

Miss Walleton stares him down, then walks past the rest of them and out the door. Brett's shoulders drop in disappointment. Kyrose sees Brett flustered and begins to flap his head and hands about, mocking Miss Walleton. They all get a kick out of him and laugh out loud.

Serana speaks up again. "Brett, you don't have to rush to go check his vitals anyway. Dr. Zazio's in there with Mr. Garner now. You can drag it on for a while and go in after he leaves."

When Serana mentioned that Dr. Zazio was with Bruce right now, once she said those words it was as if a strange vibe, strong and silent, came over the room. This vibe takes complete control, almost like a deadly snake sneaking around full of curiosity. Elizabeth heard what she said, and in thought, looks at her notepad in her grasp. She then spits out, "So Dr. Zazio's talking to Bruce right now?"

"Yes. He schedules regular visits with all the patients, of course." Serana walks past Elizabeth and out to the hallway. Elizabeth follows and looks to the end of the hall at Bruce's door. Serana walks down the hall in the opposite direction.

She stops and looks back to Elizabeth; Elizabeth is stopped in place, looking down the hall. Serana tries to get her attention. "Hey, are you going to his room?"

"I don't know. I want to hear what they're talking about. If anything," Elizabeth manages to mutter out. Serana stops and watches her for a brief second.

"Okay, I have to find Miss Walleton. I'll see you in a bit." Serana turns and walks over to Robert's room, where Miss Walleton is already working. Elizabeth still just stares at the door at the end of the hallway.

She looks back to Serana, but she's already gone. Elizabeth turns back, facing Bruce's room.

***

Bruce sits up on his bed, wearing his straightjacket and a terrible smile. Along with this hideous smile that spreads across his face, and unnaturally staring off. Right now, Bruce glares aimlessly at the white padded wall to his right. Dr. Zazio's voice is nonexistent to him; Bruce just stares.

It is clear, Bruce isn't even in there anymore. He is only a shell with wandering eyes. His eyes don't seem to fix or settle on anything that is until he gets interrupted by Dr. Zazio's voice calling to him. "Bruce! Bruce?"

The doctor yells, trying to get Bruce's attention, and it works. Bruce's eyes are really foggy and glazed over. He looks at Dr. Zazio with his drool-covered smile. Wide-eyed enlightenment overcomes Dr. Zazio, and with complete confidence returns the smile.

He looks at his notes in a fluster, amazed he even got Bruce's attention. Dr. Zazio gets more comfortable and continues on, fully knowing he has Bruce's attention. "Bruce, are you aware you have been awake for eight days now? You haven't slept; can you hear me, Bruce?"

Bruce looks to him while his eyes try to gain control, like the truth hit Bruce hard, hard enough to get a clear response from him. Bruce's jaw drops, and he shakes his head and looks around. Dr. Zazio tilts his head and awaits any form of response from the googly-eyed Bruce. Then he makes eye contact. Bruce, with his eyes swelling with tears, looks to the doctor.

Dr. Zazio continues throwing the truth in Bruce's face. "Yes, eight days now. I know you feel out of it, clearly, but can you tell me anything? Anything that you feel?"

Bruce looks dazed, and when he looks away it's clear that he is actually in thought. He looks confused while his eyes wander.

He gets loopy and his body tilts over a little. His body is fighting to hold itself up.

It's clear, he wants to fall over. Dr. Zazio watches this behavior and gets the impression he's dizzy. Dr. Zazio thinks deeply while studying Bruce. Maybe it's all the questions; maybe it's the fact of knowing the truth.

Dr. Zazio continues on, asking his questions. "Are these questions getting you dizzy? Light-headed? Maybe having to think is the cause?"

A raspy voice answers the question. "Dizzy? Oh no, not too much." Dr. Zazio is amazed to get any form of response.

This clearly proves Bruce still has brain activity. Dr. Zazio responds with a small thrill, "What was that?"

"Dizzy. I'm not dizzy. I'm not dizzy. Eight days? That is truly amazing."

"Bruce? How do you feel?"

"Not good, it's impossible to stay in control of myself. I feel myself being taken away. My memory is not here. I've been gone."

Bruce sits up and lets his head fall back, hitting the padded wall. He looks down his line of vision and locks eyes with Dr. Zazio. Bruce watches him as they look at each other in confusion. Dr. Zazio continues on with Bruce.

"You've been here, Bruce. You know you've been here with us." Bruce doesn't move; he sits and stares. Then a small thud comes from inside his straightjacket.

There's a small thump, and then another.

Dr. Zazio sees Bruce twitch and flick his hand in the jacket. Then Bruce replies, "No. I was gone. I don't know how long I've even been here. I don't even know how long I've been gone."

Bruce's eyes roll into the back of his head. Then his head rolls to the side and then rolls back. Dr. Zazio tries to keep this conversation going. "Bruce? What are your thoughts after being awake for eight days? Bruce are you still with me?"

There doesn't seem to be any response coming from him, but a ray of hope comes through once he lifts his head with pure fear in his eyes. Bruce turns his head back to the doctor. "I've been gone. I'm not in control! It's overtaken me!"

"What has?"

"What was here while I was away?" The eye contact remains between the two. Bruce's confusion was built into his statement. It drops Dr. Zazio's stomach.

Bruce leans forward to the doctor and says, "I don't know where I'm going, but I'm being taken away from here." They get interrupted by a *bang* on the door. The bang is followed by a small *buzzer*. Bruce leans back, and with a small fight, takes a deep breath and then swallows hard.

The *buzzer* goes off again. Dr. Zazio puts his notes down irritated as he doesn't like to be bothered. He looks back, then gets up from his seat and opens the door to the room. Brett stands and smiles.

Dr. Zazio looks disgruntled and sternly tells Brett, "Five minutes." Dr. Zazio goes to shut the door and in the corner of his eye sees Elizabeth down the hallway. Elizabeth watches the door shut behind Dr. Zazio.

Bruce sits up and shakes a little; it's clear he's trying to hold himself up. He manages to hold his head up and looks at the doctor. Dr. Zazio goes to speak but is cut off and distracted by a *buzz* once more. Dr. Zazio takes a deep breath.

In complete frustration, he turns around with the intention of unloading on Brett. He swings the door open but no Brett. Elizabeth is the only one standing in the doorway. The door swings open a little further, and Bruce sees her but stops and looks down, confused.

Elizabeth is greeted by Dr. Zazio while she looks in and makes eye contact with Bruce. Bruce can't hold back and shouts aloud, cutting Dr. Zazio off completely. Bruce, incomplete confusion, not sure what's going on cries out to Elizabeth.

"Elizabeth! Elizabeth! How long have I been here?" Elizabeth is a little shaken and not sure what to expect from him, but he's crying out to her. She comes in the room and pushes aside Dr. Zazio.

She quickly responds, "You've been awake eight days. You don't remember?" Elizabeth can see the pure confusion and fear in Bruce's eyes. She is terrified for him.

This is the first time in a long time she can actually see

Bruce. But it's fear's show right now, and Bruce is the main actor.

Bruce looks to the doctor and then around the room and back to Elizabeth, completely coherent.

"This can't be. I wasn't here; I've been gone! I've been gone!"

Dr. Zazio tries to get more sense out of Bruce, but Bruce only replies, "I'm not in control; I can't think, and I can't remember! I'm not in control!"

Dr. Zazio is caught off guard with this. "What do you mean you don't have control?" Bruce pauses and freezes up. Looking at them, he drops his head in agony and then in silence.

Elizabeth's stomach drops, and it's like the air in the room gets thicker and changes. She looks at Bruce. "Bruce, tell us how we can help." Elizabeth is pleading in pure agony.

Bruce lifts his head in a docile state, then leans up against the wall and replies in a terrifying voice. "Sleep, a passive, dominant part of our lives, and when we don't sleep, we fall victim to such a large dominant part that is highly unknown to any of you." Bruce gets cut off by himself when he starts to shake and quiver. Then he stops, but they all stop once Bruce lets out a gut-dropping roar!

It seems to put the entire hospital to a halt. And like it never happened, silence comes again. Bruce goes silent, then his body begins to convulse. He convulses so hard it appears something's attempting to rip out of his chest.

Elizabeth watches in fear, but she has to be on her game, so she runs to the door and swings it open and yells out to the help.

"Brett! Nurses! We need a hand in here. Code 3!"

Dr. Zazio tries to calm Bruce by standing by his side with his hand over his chest. "Breathe, Bruce… Bruce, breathe. We need to take this jacket off to get to his chest!" Brett rushes into the room to help them and they start undoing the straps to the jacket.

Bruce convulses harder and starts to foam from his mouth. Elizabeth stands back, a little out of breath, as the white jacket gets taken off and is slid across the floor. Bruce convulses harder, too hard for the doctor and the nurse to contain him. Bruce twists hard and falls off the bed onto the floor.

He heaves and scratches out to the middle of the floor. He reaches out, then very quickly slides to the corner of the room in a small ball, covering his face. All seems to be quiet and still. Silence only for the moment, but they are all caught off guard when Bruce stands straight up, tall and wide.

He speaks in a voice that is abnormal and certainly not his own. "I am immortally insane! I have or will imperium all of you." The look Bruce gives them proves that their eyes can produce haunting images never to be forgotten.

Dr. Zazio rushes over and grabs the jacket, and Brett gets on guard in a clearly "trained for this situation" stance.

Dr. Zazio is actually keeping calm and is almost welcoming to the circumstance. "Now Bruce…"

Dr. Zazio gets cut off by this man standing in the corner of the padded room. "Lynol!"

The light above him in the corner of the room goes out. Dr. Zazio is a little taken back but agrees. "Okay. Lynol, put your arms out. I know you don't want to hurt us. Let's put this jacket back on."

Bruce looks to Elizabeth; he smiles so big it looks painful. Elizabeth's stomach drops. Bruce just stands watching them, then he puts his arms up in a twitchy manner. He points his arms out and points his drooped wrist toward them from the corner of the room. They're all speechless and a little taken back.

Then, in a fast, twitchy motion, he moves out of the corner toward Dr. Zazio. Dr. Zazio stands his ground and can see Bruce is being cooperative with them. He slides the jacket over his arms quickly straps it tight. Bruce hasn't taken his eyes off Elizabeth, and they stretch open wider and wider.

Dr. Zazio and Brett take him to his bed. Bruce keeps his attention locked on Elizabeth. She watches him in complete confusion as a teardrop falls from her eye. Dr. Zazio attempts to continue on with the conversation, and he tries to get Bruce's attention off Elizabeth. "Lynol? Lynol?" Bruce takes his eyes off Elizabeth and directs his attention slowly and creepily, to Dr. Zazio. Elizabeth tears up and lets out a sob.

Once again, she has all of Bruce's attention, and with a raspy voice he says, "Aw, don't be sad."

Dr. Zazio, trying to get his attention, raises his voice once again at him. "Lynol! Answer me." Bruce turns to Dr. Zazio with his eyes lost and dark. They get wider, even though you might think it's impossible. He gives the doctor a terrifying look. Brett is traumatized.

Bruce shakes a little, and more foam escapes his mouth. He continues to turn his head back to Elizabeth, locking eyes with her. Elizabeth is shaken, and Lynol speaks up.

"Elizabeth. When was the last time you slept? Because I can see into you, and I know the entity that resides in your flesh on this day. You might want to sleep and rid yourself of him. He's not a good one."

His voice is deep and unnatural. Her heart skips a beat and a vibe comes over her she feels completely out of control of her body. A shock of negative energy shakes her and she turns and runs out of the room. Bruce looks to Dr. Zazio and Brett and smiles.

Elizabeth leaves the room, rushing out of the doorway. She can't handle the gibberish and the madness that is pouring out of Bruce. Elizabeth doesn't know how he does it, but Bruce seems to be able to peek into the darkest part of her soul. Elizabeth is already out the door into the hallway, but she is still freaking out a little.

She can't take it after the words he spoke. Her head feels heavy, like all she wants to do is sleep. Elizabeth paces towards the stairs. She tries to collect herself and her thoughts, but a faint noise comes from behind her.

A simple grunt comes out of Bruce's room at the end of the hall. Elizabeth hears this and picks up the pace like the stairs couldn't come quick enough. Elizabeth's imagination gets the best of her and she sprints to the light at the end of the hallway, which is beaming down on the staircase. She sprints like she's getting chased.

Elizabeth makes it up the stairs and instantly slows down her pace but keeps on walking. She makes her way into the break room. Dr. Holden sits drinking his coffee, looking over his notes. He gets distracted by Elizabeth coming around the corner in a panic.

She keeps looking behind her, but it's playing against her advantage because she almost trips over his foot while he sits. Dr. Holden can see she's pale and not at all coherent. Holden doesn't take his eyes off his paper and then takes a sip of his coffee. Elizabeth looks to the far wall of this break room and sees a dark green sofa with a silver armrest sitting in the back up against the wall.

It looks like the best place to take a nap. Elizabeth rushes over and throws herself on it. She gets ever so comfortable and kicks her feet up. She rolls her head tries her best to go to sleep.

Holden has his attention still set on the paper. "Elizabeth?"

"Yeah."

"Are you okay?" Dr. Holden lifts his eyes from the paper and watches her struggle to get comfortable on the break room couch. She rolls back over and looks at Holden sitting quietly with a concerned look on his face. Elizabeth, with a dazed over set of thoughts, speaks up.

"I'm just trying to go to sleep. I feel something in me…something."

"Like a parasite?"

"No, like a negative force that I can't control. I want to wash away this moment."

"Then sleep."

"I want to wash away this moment." Elizabeth locks eyes with Dr. Holden with a silent scream for help.

She continues, "Like I need to clean myself, refresh myself…am I going mad?" Elizabeth ends up trailing off in the conversation but is completely trying to help him understand her situation in any sense.

Dr. Holden looks at her to continue. "No, of course not. Elizabeth…" He gets cut off by Dr. Zazio walking around the corner, up from the lower level. He looks at Dr. Holden, then sees Elizabeth lying down with her arm over her face, distraught.

Dr. Zazio, trying to be of some comfort, says, "I left Brett with Bruce. Are you okay?" Dr. Zazio's awkwardness doesn't help Elizabeth cope whatsoever. Elizabeth sits up and takes her feet off the couch.

She leans forward, winded, with her head in her hands. Miss. Walleton and Serana come up into the break room behind Dr. Zazio. "What's up with all the commotion?" Simon comes out of the security office and asks.

***

The door swings open to Bruce's room, with Brett cautiously on the other end. Brett pushes the door the rest of the way open until it hits the wall. He slowly peeks his head in the room and sees Bruce sitting in the dark corner with a terrible smile spread across his face. Brett swallows hard and decides he needs to get this over with, quick.

Brett goes into the room and then for some off-the-wall reason, Bruce changes his reaction. The creepy smile goes away, and he smiles like a regular man coyly. Bruce leans his head back up against the wall with an off sense of confidence. If he had some sunglasses, he would be wearing them.

Instantly, the one light flickers back on. With Bruce leaning up against the back wall, the vibe calms in the room. Brett even seems to let his guard down. He looks over to Bruce.

"Come on, let's get these vitals done, and I'll let you get back to relaxing. If you would please stand up, I need to remove your jacket to get to your arms." Bruce smiles a chill smile at Brett and rocks a little, trying to get his balance. Bruce stands and turns his back to him, implying to take off the jacket.

Brett holds his chart, confused over Bruce's complete cooperation and understanding. Brett looks up to the camera that is staring them in the face and lets out a little shrug. Brett assumes maybe he's been over-thinking this entire situation. Bruce stands facing the wall and says in a calm voice, "It's amazing the cool, calm feeling you can bring over your body at any given time."

Brett comes over with his confidence high, for some odd reason, and goes up to the buckles on the back of

Bruce's jacket. Brett puts his clipboard under his arm and fights with the buckle until he stops and throws the clipboard on the bed next to the open door. Brett is not really listening as Bruce jabbers on. "I still can't believe the power of this thing. I mean, the strength."

Brett fights with the buckles, then Bruce stretches his arms out with force. His movement catches Brett off guard. The buckle unlatches, and the jacket is loose. Brett jumps back, a little confused. "Okay. Let's just finish. I'm going to need your right arm." Brett looks around and notices he left the medicine cart out in the hallway. Brett bends over and grabs his clipboard and continues, "I need to get my medicine cart, then I'll need that arm."

Brett looks to Bruce, who is still facing the corner. Then like a flash, Bruce flips around in a nerve-racking way but still looks chill and calm. He drops his arms, facing Brett. Brett doesn't know how to respond to him but tries to keep his composure.

Brett turns away from him and goes out to the hallway where he left his cart. Brett leans on the cart and takes a deep breath, whispering to himself, "All right, just do the vitals and get out of that damn room." He clenches his fists up and rolls the cart into the room. Bruce is still standing in the corner, exactly how Brett left him.

Brett can't make eye contact with him; it's the most off-putting thing. Brett tries to finish and do his job. "Bruce, if you could come over here and I will help you take off the jacket." Bruce takes a second, then slowly paces to the middle of the room where Brett patiently and fearfully waits.

Bruce has different vibes attached to him; the waves come and go. Brett can feel every single one of them as they radiate off of Bruce. He walks up to him with a vacant expression. Brett takes a breath and helps one of Bruce's arms, out of the straightjacket.

Once Bruce has his one free arm out, he forces it straight into the air, out of Brett's grasp. He reaches for the sky, and then he stops and looks over his own arm in complete amazement. His arm's a mess with dried blood on the forearm, and his fingers are chewed up. Bruce just smiles when he sees his hand out in the open and has to say, "The pain is very physical. It's actually easy to shut down that law of the body."

Brett watches him look over his hand in such amazement like he's never seen it before. Then, a creepy smile begins to make its way back across Bruce's face. Brett tries to get his attention and grabs his hand and calmly talks him down. "Now, all I need is to make sure your heart rate and all of your vitals are okay. Then we can get Miss Walleton in here to look at your hand and fingers."

Brett is caught off guard with Bruce's rambling. He reaches over and pulls a stethoscope off his cart and tries to get Bruce's attention. Bruce is still in love with his hand. Brett watches him, then grabs his arms and body and attempts to sit him down on the bed.

Brett tries to gain control. "Now, let me finish. Bruce, sit down." Bruce sits down on the bed with a thud. Brett is caught off guard when the door slams shut behind him.

The vibe in the room does a one-eighty, and it's gone completely negative. It's Lynol. He frowns and gets very serious, with a raspy cold response. "Lynol. I'm sure that's what you meant to say?"

Brett looks back to the door and has complete fear come over him. He turns back to Bruce as his other hand comes out from the straightjacket. Then all the lights flicker out while Lynol smiles.

***

Dr. Zazio stands up straight, with his hands behind his back, looking down on Elizabeth. Miss Walleton stands on his right-hand side awaiting his command. Dr. Zazio leans over and whispers to Miss Walleton, "I have this; please go see if Brett needs a hand." Elizabeth adjusts herself, clears her nose, and replies.

"I'm just really shaken over all this…I mean, what are we going to do? He needs to sleep." She puts up her hands and leans forward like she is at her wit's end. It's clear, she's silently begging for help.

Dr. Zazio has some sort of cold, heartless look spread across his face while he is staring down at her. Holden puts his drink aside while he sits on the arm of the chair. He sees Elizabeth in a struggle and stands up and attempts to calm her. "I'm heading down to the lab now. I have some ideas going on about how I think I can get him to sleep."

Dr. Zazio turns back to him with a look of curiosity in his eyes. Serana sits on the couch and scoots over and grabs Elizabeth. She tries to calm her, "Calm down. The doctors are doing all they can to help him, I promise."

Elizabeth calms a little, giving over her trust, and then they both lean back on the sofa. Holden comes around and stands next to Dr. Zazio. Holden tries to get his point across "We know he needs sleep, but this is very difficult to do, especially considering the circumstances and the fact that his blood rejects all the medicine and medical ways possible to put him down."

Dr. Zazio continues to stand upright, with his hands behind his back, looking down on them and not wanting to contribute to the conversation. Dr. Zazio continues his own rant. "Now Elizabeth, we need to continue our process, and I was sure that you had told me you weren't going to let Bruce's condition affect you like this. That is why I brought you along and into my hospital in the first place."

Elizabeth looks up to the doctor, not sure how to respond to him. Dr. Zazio gives off such a negative vibe – almost heartless. She pushes her tears aside and looks up to him. Holden drops his hands and goes back to the arm of the chair and his drink.

He takes in a deep breath; he knows he needs to find some way to put Bruce to sleep. Deep down, he knows one of his ideas that he's working on is destined to work. Elizabeth watches Dr. Zazio, and only one thing comes to mind that she wants to say. She speaks up.

"What is Lynol?"

Dr. Zazio pauses and looks to Elizabeth and replies with a chuckle. "It's what he said his name was." *Whirl*! *Whirl*!

An alarm blares loud, and once again, the room and everyone in it becomes a disaster as they all jump up and take the cornerback down to the hospital. Simon rushes to check the monitors in the security room.

The other four of them rush down from the break room, running down the stairs into the lower part of the hospital and down to the sounds of panic as the alarm blares. Miss Walleton is smashing her fist on the alarm button in the hallway. She hears the alarms, but it doesn't stop her. It's clear she's in a panic, as she continues to smash her hand into the panic button with no remorse.

Her other hand is covering her mouth in complete terror. She stops, stumbles to the side, and falls to the ground. She lets out a scream that echoes through the hallway and looks back to the four people rushing up with terror in her eyes. Bruce's door is slightly cracked open at the end of the hall.

Elizabeth sees it, but it seems like it is miles away. Simon makes his way through the break room and then turns the corner to the staircase. He rushes down the steps as he hears the breathtaking scream come from Miss Walleton. He picks up the pace and everything comes into view.

The crew rushes to the end of the hall. Miss Walleton, in a panic, manages to get on her feet. Before a word is spoken, she starts to powerwalk the opposite way, past Dr. Zazio and the crew that was rushing toward her. Simon comes down into the hallway and Miss Walleton rushes past him with rivers of tears coming out of her eyes.

Simon turns around and watches her run up the stairs away from everyone. He turns back toward the room at the end of the hall. Holden rushes past Dr. Zazio and up to the cracked open door. He is the first to get to the door and, with all his might, tries to force it open.

It feels like there is something very heavy stopping the door from opening. Holden tries harder and harder, but the door doesn't budge. Instead, the door gets pushed closed with ease as if Holden wasn't trying to push it open at all. The crew looks over the door in confusion.

Then Simon comes running up. Holden stops and turns to Simon. "The door pushed back as if someone is in there someone pushing it closed." Holden turns back to the door and pushes with all his might.

Simon and the rest of the group join in, and they all force the door open. The door swings open and Holden is the first one in the room. He instantly turns pale. The rest of them make their way in a panic.

Elizabeth almost faints. The white padded room is speckled with blood, and in the far corner, no white can be seen. The only white is the white of the back of Bruce's shirt as he sits with his head down facing the corner…holding and eating half of Brett's bloody body. Elizabeth and Serana fall in a panic.

Holden looks away. He then looks around the room and behind the door to see what was stopping them from opening it, but to his surprise, there is nothing there. He sees the other half of Brett's body on the bed. Elizabeth yells in a panic, "Bruce! What are you doing?"

Lynol stops with his back turned to them, standing in a creepy manner. He rises with no effort, higher and higher, till he is on the tips of his toes. Then in a flash, he turns and faces them. The front of him is drenched in blood.

He makes eye contact, not blinking, and then slowly raises his arms out to his sides. The inside of his arms is scratched away. It is clear Brett was fighting him. Elizabeth can't take it and runs out of the room, passing the straightjacket that lies in a bloody mess up against the wall. His smile takes them all by surprise.

He still stands up tall and on his toes. They go to grab him, and he laughs out loud. He extends both arms toward them and the door flings closed. Elizabeth is out in the hall as she turns around in a shock, looking at the door.

She hears another few bangs in the distance; things are slamming down all around the hospital. All of their stomachs drop, and while laughing, Bruce reaches out and then up…and begins to rip his own eyes out of their sockets.

Chapter 11
May 18th and 23rd, 1998 – 2:45 P.M.
(The Video)

Elizabeth has her head up while talking to the courtroom. She is watching the room full of listeners cower away from the story. "After that, of course, no one wanted to go near him." Elizabeth gets a little shaken in her seat, still on the stand.

It took a minute before the emotion to hit her again, and Elizabeth isn't sure if her becoming numb is a good thing. She swallows hard and wipes her nose, and continues. "We had to restrain him and watch him. Well, you know…keep an eye on him." The prosecutor stands, shaking his head at Elizabeth, raises his hand to his mouth. It's clear, the prosecutor is going to question her. The prosecutor is clearly in doubt over her emotion that is tied along with her story. He turns to the courtroom still in thought.

"So, when you say the door just closed?" The prosecutor says it with a voice that sends a bad vibe to Elizabeth; makes her skin crawl. The tone of his voice leaves a bad taste in her mouth. Elizabeth lashes out.

"Yeah, it closed! I'm sure you've seen the tapes." Elizabeth almost lifts off her seat. She calmly looks to the judge and then back to the prosecutor.

The prosecutor gets on the defense and throws his hands up! "Wow, calm down. Calm down this isn't that place." He turns to walk back to his table.

Elizabeth takes in a deep breath, fed up. She slouches down in her seat. The prosecutor grabs the zipper of his bag that so casually sits on the chair. He opens it the rest of the way and then digs inside.

"If you want to bring out the tapes, we can do that."

The prosecutor pulls out a small camera from inside the bag. "Yes, we can. We can play one of those videos, right now."

He holds the camera high in the air then a little *click* and the videotape pops out. The prosecutor puts down the camera and grabs the tape. He turns and walks up to the judge's stand, and puts the tape down and taps on it. He then nods to the judge.

The judge looks at the smug prosecutor and rolls his eyes. Then calls over the officer standing off to the side of the courtroom, with a nod. The officer walks up and grabs the tape off of his desk. The officer mumbles something under his breath, along the lines of "Rrrrplugrrr in thrrr tvrr." The judge looks at him with a stern stare. He walks over to the TV set up. The cables already clearly labeled, and all the officer is trying to do is plug it in.

He finds the right cable, but of course, it's tangled. He grunts and fights with it; he even drops to one knee. The officer places the tape on the ground, while he fights with the cables. The prosecutor runs up and picks up the tape.

The officer manages to plug the television in. The prosecutor helps him up to his feet. The officer takes the tape and slides it in. The prosecutor looks to the room and it's clear the screen has everyone's attention.

The officer reaches over to the video player and presses, play. The prosecutor speaks up quickly, "Now to warn you. This is a vulgar video. I warn anyone not wanting to witness this, to look away."

Having seen the video from that gruesome night, the prosecutor is quick to look away, himself. He turns and with his back to the screen continues talking to the crowd. "This is a video that concludes Miss Primrose's story." The video begins, and it's bloody and vulgar, but yet so hard for anyone to look away.

Elizabeth looks down and away, along with anyone who has already seen it. The video is loud and Brett's screams are more than real. With a flash, Bruce rips out his own eyes. The room pulls back and looks away.

A grotesque memory that now may never go away. In the video; it's clear that the door closes on its own. The crowd or the one's still watching gasp in horror, followed with an uncontrolled reaction to seeing the door close by itself. The judge tries to gain control.

"Silence! Silence."

He turns to the officer. "Replay that. In slow motion, if you can." The officer grabs the remote and the audience is once again silent with every eye on the screen.

They replay the tape of the door being pushed closed. Then again, and again. Elizabeth relieved, they got to see that on tape. The prosecutor is a little pale, even though he's seen the video.

The judge waves the officer to stop. "That's enough turn it off."

The officer obeys and the prosecutor continues on, "Well there you have it, ladies and gentleman."

The officer turns off the television and places the video on the judge's stand. He walks back to the other side of the room. The prosecutor walks back up to Elizabeth on the stand and tries to get a grasp on what she's been through. "So, you were clearly terrified, afraid, and lost hope?"

Elizabeth without hesitation speaks up, "No! I never lost hope."

"What? How could you continue? He was already doing damage to himself and clearly others. What were the steps you were taking to help him?"

"Dr. Holden was putting together a way to put him to sleep. That's what we focused on, a way to put him to sleep." Elizabeth is confident she was trying to do the right thing, all along. For the first time in this trial the prosecutor lets up, or so it seems.

The prosecutor continues on his part of the interrogation. "So, after this?"

"After Dr. Zazio cleared up everything, for the time being, we were still trying to treat Bruce."

"You guys brought in a new nurse, correct?"

Elizabeth's expression drops and all the buried memories come straight up to the surface. "Yes, we got a new nurse. A stronger nurse to say the least, Mr. Sturino."

"Thomas Sturino."

"Yes."

Elizabeth tears up and looks over the courtroom and over the crowd listening. She can't fight it back even though she really wants to. These memories are cutting her up, and it all comes on strong. "Yes, Dr. Zazio hired him and brought him on."

"What happened?"

"Well, he was being a hero, alongside Simon…" Elizabeth tears up too much, it's hard for her to catch her breath. She puts her hand up for a brief pause and the judge bends down and pats her on the back. The judge puts up his hand to the prosecutor and holds off the questioning for a moment. Elizabeth sits up straight and tries to pull it together.

***

The laboratory is dark, it's always dark. A dark blue fills the room with only curtain stations lit up by a direct extreme amount of light, shining down on them. Holden sits in one of these stations, looking through an instrument. He can see clearly into the glasses of the microscope.

What he looks at is getting bigger and bigger. Holden has his grasp on a lime green softball. He squeezes it tight. He holds his breath hopes to keep the image clear, long enough to be able to analyze it correctly.

Holden switches lenses and at the same time unknowingly switches to his other eye. He throws the ball behind his back to his other hand. He looks deeper into the microscope. It brings to life the clarity of the situation, but the deeper he looks, unfortunately, the deeper his own thoughts go with an entirely different analysis of himself.

He gets distrait over the entire thing; this entire situation. He needs to figure all of this out. He believes,

Bruce was once a real, good man, not a killer. He doesn't deserve any of this.

Holden's thoughts get the best of him, and he has to let go of the microscope before he messes things up. He let go, and then abruptly falls back on the chair behind him. He needs a breather. Holden throws the lime green ball in the air, but the beaming light blinds him.

While he sits back in his seat. He catches the ball and then puts the ball on his table. He rubs both of his eyes. The thought is stuck, now along with the new set of horrible memories.

Holden hopes he can fix all of this. So, he can at least have a good finish to the set of already shitty memories. Holden looks down at his cluttered desk. His eyes still adjusting to the dark blue that hoovers behind the blinding light.

He looks at the microscope and decides to give his eyes a small break. He scans over his cluttered table, and over the different medications he has out in front of him. Picks up a tiny medicine bottle and looks it over. He puts it down and then picks up another one.

The door opens and gives off heavy scrapping of metal, type of sound. The noise breaks Holden's concentration. Holden sits upright and grasps the little bottle of medicine. The door swings the rest of the way open, it's Elizabeth.

She peeks in and sees Holden in the distance; the light beams on him. The dark blue is gloomy in this room. It also seems slightly colder than the rest of the hospital. Elizabeth walks in and interrupts Holden's thought process.

Holden places the tiny medicine bottle back down on his cluttered table. He looks to her and wonders why

Elizabeth came into this room, but he already knows the answer. Elizabeth makes her way into the room, and over to Dr. Holden. "You close? To find out anything?"

Dr. Holden grabs his notebook off his desk and looks a few things over. Elizabeth comes in, "Doctor? Anything?" She wants to talk, and he can tell she's distraught.

She's only trying to be productive. Dr. Holden leans back and with a deep sigh. "Yes, actually." Elizabeth almost stops dead in her tracks.

Elizabeth comes into the conversation, "Really?" The simple statement puts a shed of hope in her heart, it almost brings her back to life.

"Now, my prediction is serum adenosine. It will work. It's a chemical in your blood that builds up the blood cells. It helps thicken the blood to make the body go to sleep." Holden talks with his hands.

Elizabeth quick to reply, "Yes, I've actually heard of it."

Dr. Holden continues on with his theory. "Well, we will mix it with a blood-coagulant. We mix the two into Bruce's bloodstream and this will help put him to sleep."

"Well hopefully before he can force it out of his system." Elizabeth still in a daze, paces around.

"Do you think it will really work? Is there a possibility this could kill him?"

"A small chance, but if so, then moments after it kicks in and he falls asleep. We will need to induce a stabilizer, to reduce his blood pressure. It's well worth a try."

"If you're positive about this then we need to do it quickly." Holden gets up and stands next to Elizabeth trying to make her feel more confident and continues.

"We will, but I need to finish some more tests and studies. I'm rushing, trust me."

She can see the passion that Dr. Holden has. He turns and goes back to his seat, leaving Elizabeth with a height of new confidence and hope. Dr. Holden gave it to her with hope in his eyes, overcoming the fear of the entire situation.

Elizabeth smiles; the first time in a long time. She is actually smiling. She gets up and walks around the room; observing everything. Elizabeth paces back and forth.

Holden leans forward and looks back into the microscope.

She watches him work, then with an urge to ask, even over the guilt. "What do you think of Lynol?" Holden looks up at her from the viewing lens with a stern expression spread across his face.

He leans back in his chair and puts his arms up over his head. Holden first takes a deep breath and then responds. "That's a tough one. A very sensitive subject. Do you want my honest opinion or…?"

He gets cut off by Elizabeth. She grabs the closest lab stool and is now sliding it up to his table. Elizabeth stops and sits, "I want you to be completely honest, about everything that is happening?" Elizabeth with a very curious voice, she is clearly an avid listener.

Elizabeth makes herself comfortable sitting next to Holden. He looks around the darkroom for a second and then looks back at Elizabeth.

"Bruce hasn't slept for eleven days going on twelve. I am honestly surprised he is even alive. I'm sure that they let Dr. Zazio keep him down here after his incident because they all believe he should be dead by now. And Lynol? I think he is just an alter ego, created for survival on Bruce's part."

The coyness of Dr. Holden shines bright while he sits back. He continues, "Or Lynol is a spirit or an entity of some sort. Something that is attempting to steal the body away from Bruce. Maybe simply over the fact that it doesn't have one of its own."

Elizabeth's stomach drops and her eyes get a little watery.

She looks away into the darkness surrounding them. She feels the cold drift all around. Holden sits up and can see he's upsetting her.

He begins to fiddles with the microscope and slightly changes the subject. "I don't think so though. Because, let's take Robert, the schizo. And his friend just to add to the oddness…Spingolia. Have you had a chance to sit and talk with him? Or them?"

Elizabeth tries to understand where he is going with this, but she replies with a dainty and fragile voice. "No, I haven't really sat down and talked to him alone, but I think I understand his situation."

"Well if you get a chance, sit with him."

"How does he act?" Holden still fiddles and looks up to Elizabeth.

"The brain is a very powerful thing. Robert will actively and physically cut himself. He would then say, it was Spingolia that did it. The funny thing about it all is we've never seen him actually do it…cut himself.

Yet, he is clearly cut. Most of the time when it happens Robert appears terrified. He's consciously afraid of something that is there with him. So, with Lynol, being a survival alter ego. I don't know, sometimes I don't know where any of these things come from. Lynol or Spingolia. Maybe it's an alternate reality forcing its way through us."

A cold chill fills the room as Dr. Holden finishes his sentence. Elizabeth takes it all in, but Dr. Holden even went further than he wanted to. He needs to clear the air. "Bruce will be back after he sleeps."

Dr. Holden gets up and paces back and forth in deep thought. Elizabeth watches him. He stops and then begins on another rant. "Let's say you are always sleepy, but the neurons of your brain keep you awake."

Elizabeth gives off a very confused look, but Dr. Holden continues. "The neurons keep you awake by delivering emotions to you. Emotions tied with certain chemicals, like Serotonin and so on. So, in reality, the body is always falling asleep, but your brain activity keeps you filled with emotion, causing the human body to stay awake to experience it. Almost like an obligation."

Dr. Holden stops in his tracks and then realizes one thing. "Lynol. He keeps all the brain activity going. He will not stop, forcing Bruce to be alive, awake." Elizabeth is slightly confused but wants to feed into Holden's thoughts.

"But doing this will ultimately lead to killing the body."

Dr. Holden sits back down in his chair. "Correct and the thing that gets me with Lynol is he looks at Bruce as another being, not human. That's where I lose my conclusion."

Holden goes into deep thought and trails off. Elizabeth stands up walking around tries to understand. She feels fed up and tired. She notices six different bottles in front of Holden, on his table.

Holden watches Elizabeth's expression change once she looks at the bottles. She overlooks the serums, and notices there are three of one kind, and three of another. Holden watches Elizabeth's reaction to the bottles as she reads the labels. Three of the bottles read, "Adenosine."

The other three just have small print and numbers on the label, #2544. Elizabeth clearly remembers the conversation and has to ask. "The adenosine is to put him to sleep, right? Once mixed with other chemicals. Then what are these other three bottles for? The other chemicals?"

Holden leans back in his chair and almost doesn't want to reply, but he does. "Those are Dr. Zazio's formulas. He is trying to replicate a serum with the same effects. The same effects that will help keep a person awake for long periods of time."

Elizabeth gets a disgusted look over her face and is about to lash out. But they are both interrupted by the *screeching* sound of someone opening the door. They both turn simultaneously to see who's walking in. Simon peeks his head in the room and sees the two of them at the table.

He waves, "Sorry to interrupt, but I think you guys need to see something." Simon has a confused look spread across his face. Holden jumps up and they head out the door.

The three of them make their way out into the dark hallway. It gives off a cold, chilling feeling. All three stand in the middle of the hallway. Simon faces the two of them.

The lab's door closes behind them, and Dr. Holden and Elizabeth look at Simon patiently waiting for him to show them what was so important. Simon looks very uneasy. He takes a deep breath and sighs a little. It's clear something's wrong.

"What is it, Simon?" Elizabeth asked, with care in her voice. Simon looks to his right, straight at Bruce's door. Holden looks at him with a bit of concern.

Simon shakes his head and manages to mutter out. "It's Bruce, he's acting weird." Holden looks over to Bruce's room, slowly walks to the door. It's dead silent. Elizabeth and Simon walk behind him, following.

Holden reaches the door and goes to look into Bruce's room with anxiety spread across his entire skeleton. His hands grasp the door's window. He looks inside completely. The other two follow and step up to look in also.

Bruce is standing, wide-awake leaned up against the wall. Elizabeth looks in again. Bruce walks over to the far corner and ever so slowly sits on the floor, with his bandaged face to the wall. His arms clearly moving inside the straightjacket, still awake.

Holden turns and walks away. Simon confused over this looks back in the window. Simon shakes his head. "No, no."

Dr. Holden socks him in the arm walking by. "Come on Simon stop messing around. You don't have a fitness magazine or something to be looking at?" Elizabeth and Simon turn around, and you can literally see Simon's shoulders drop.

Dr. Holden walks back down the hallway. "Man…he wasn't like that on the camera." Simon manages to get out his last words.

They all three go back to the lab's door and Holden swings it open.

Simon confused, but he knows something's not right. "No, wait. Bruce *is* acting weird. Let's go watch him on the camera." Holden looks to Elizabeth, considering.

Simon continues, "Come on. I wouldn't ask you guys if it wasn't important." Simon seems to plea with Dr. Holden. Then he looks back at Bruce's room with a sense of fear and panic.

Elizabeth gets the chills and speaks out, "Let's go. I need to see what he's talking about." Elizabeth turns and they walk to the staircase at the end of the hall. Simon feels a sense of back up, happy to try and put an end to this madness.

Elizabeth looks back at Holden standing stuck in purgatory; of watching the camera or burying himself back into the microscope. Holden looks into the dark lab and then turns and sees Elizabeth wave for him to follow. Holden lets the lab door *screech,* closed behind him. He runs down the hall to catch up with Simon and Elizabeth.

Simon leads the way up the stairs and around the corner, back into the break room, Elizabeth and Dr. Holden follow on his trail. There isn't anybody else around. The others must have already left for the day. Simon goes into the next doorway, then he is back home in his little security office.

Elizabeth follows Simon into his office. Dr. Holden sneaks a snack, off the table in the lounge. He throws it back into his mouth and walks into the security room. Holden almost spits the snack out.

He coughs out loud, caught off guard with what he sees on the monitor screen. Dr. Holden shocked and can't take his eyes off of the screen, locked on. What he sees is Bruce standing there, tall and looking into the camera. His head is tilted, and a smile spread across his face.

He stares at them with black, ripped-out eyes. This catches all three of them off guard. Elizabeth swears, she can feel a pain in her chest. They feel uneasy as they look at one another.

They are all three speechless, watching Bruce on the monitor. Bruce stands there and stares. Not looking at the camera, but looking at them. He backs up and they can see the straightjacket is off.

The jacket lays on the floor behind this being. This monster, smiling through the camera. As the three observe what they are witnessing. It makes the picture of their reality vanish.

Reality vanishes but is quick to come back and make all three of them sick to their stomach. Bruce has tears rolling down his clawed out, eyes. The being on the camera is twitchy. He twitches with every movement; quickly and in-human.

He moves faster around the room. Holden looks at them, "Is the video in fast forward?"

Simon hard to look away responds, "It's a live feed." Bruce is back, looking straight at them with no eyes.

Elizabeth almost passes out where she stands. "He can hear us." Silence feels the room that they are crowded into. Holden still trying to get down his food.

He hits Simon in the arm, nods to him implying for them to run down to Bruce's room. Holden knows they need to go down there. Simon watches for a second longer then nods yes, and jumps up. They run out of the room.

Elizabeth can't stay here alone. She feels the tears pour out of her eyes. She follows Simon and Dr. Holden. The two of them run down the stairs as if in a race, but they slow when they get Bruce's door in sight.

Simon has his hand clenched in a fist so tight, that he can feel his own circulation. The two of them; Simon and Dr. Holden walk down the dark hallway toward Bruce's room. Bruce's door sits unlatched and cracked open at the end of the hall. A bright light crawls out of the crack, from inside the room.

They get to the door, and Holden reaches out. He pushes the door open ever so gently. Elizabeth comes down the stairs walking up behind them watching their every move. *Bang!*

Robert slams up against his door. Robert always is trying to see what's going on. He looks out the glass at Elizabeth. She glares at him and continues toward Bruce's room.

Elizabeth is scared and it shows. She gets three-quarters of the way down the hall and stops. She comes to a stop a few feet away from the door and watches Dr. Holden. He is already pushing Bruce's door open. Simon takes a deep breath and they proceed to push it the rest of the way open and go inside.

The door lets off a loud *creak*. They enter the room. Simon and Dr. Holden walk in the room and before their eyes could adjust to the brightness, the lights flicker out. Elizabeth watches them from the hall and then darkness.

She walks over to the dark and silence, then joins them inside. Instantly when she entered the room Elizabeth gets overwhelmed with a strong odor; a terrible smell. It's a smell that will haunt you, if not hurt you. The guys already stand in the dark with their noses covered.

Elizabeth gets closer to them, makes her way into the room. Where the smell is the strongest; a rotten sweet. Holden stands tall and Simon gets on guard ready for anything. Bruce sits facing the corner.

It's dark and quiet. Simon motions to Holden that, "He has his strait-jacket back on." Elizabeth goes white when she sees the straight-jacket is even buckled up the back. Holden attempts to take charge, "Bruce, we need to talk with you. It's about the cure that we have. We have what we need to put you to sleep."

The door slowly creeps closed behind the three of them. Simon turns and watches the door close. His complexion turns as white as the wall. Holden attempts to continue but doesn't want to get too close

"Bruce? Bruce?" It's clear, he's not going to get any form of response.

Elizabeth leans forward up next to Dr. Holden and calls out to him. "Lynol!"

Instantly Bruce's body stands with his face to the wall. He stands in a way that is eerie and appears impossible to do. Elizabeth jumps back in fear she expected a reaction, but not this. Then silence.

Bruce spins around facing them in the same twitchy, fast manner. Bruce turns to her with blood spots splashed on his face.

He wears an eerie grin, and droll spills from him with his eyes clawed out. He faces all three of them and makes a comment.

"Ah, Elizabeth you've come." Lynol stares at her and throws out his arms, with the straightjacket still on. That was believed to be impossible. Holden tries to stand tall and hold his ground.

Then the lock on the door *latches* closed. All three of their stomach drops. Holden speaks out, "Now Lynol. You need to calm down."

Lynol looks toward Holden. Elizabeth whimpers, and turns to the door. She covers her face. She can actually feel her self-fighting the urge to pass out.

She reaches out for the door handle. Lynol drops his arms and the buckles in the back of his jacket unlatch, and the jacket falls to the ground. Elizabeth pulls, but the door won't open. She instantly panics.

The panic rises in her blood after hearing the jacket *cling* on the ground. Simon is doing his best to stand his ground, but fear is a hell of a thing. "Bruce put the jacket back on!" Simon yells.

Lynol looks at Simon and grins. Then in a weird twitchy motion turns around and faces the corner again, his back to them. Elizabeth is relentless to get the door open. She tugs with all her might, but nothing.

Simon thinks about helping Elizabeth with the door. He's not getting through to Bruce and he wants out of this room. Holden stands strong. Lynol faces the wall then in a twitchy motion, sits back down.

He begins to rock back and forth, and the room gets colder. It's fair to say the room is almost freezing. Bruce begins to chant in a deep voice, deeper and deeper. It sounds like grunts, instead of words. Then a *crack!*

They all three pause, the loud *crack* got all of their attention. All eyes are locked on Bruce. He sits with his back to them in the dark corner. Dr. Holden looks back at the other two in confusion.

Simon goes over to Elizabeth and he fights with the lock. Lynol continues with an odd humming. Then he grunts again and then *crack*! Dr. Holden freezes up.

So does Simon, the only one that doesn't is Elizabeth while she gives it all she's got pulling on the door. She is wanting out of the room; she tugs harder on the verge of hurting herself. Then another *crack* Holden pauses then with deep concern, and to witness the realization of what Bruce is doing.

Dr. Holden says under his breath, "He's breaking his bones." Then a ripping noise drops Holden's jaw in panic. Then another *rip*. Lynol peeks from the dark corner.

"The body can heal twice as fast as predicted when it's forced. You see. The body has so many rules, but like any great device, it can be controlled. Especially when you tear down its laws."

Lynol jumps up and swings around. The faces of the three reflect in horror. Bruce spins around and shows the true dementedness of his now, true nature. Lynol has broken the bones and stretched all the flesh from his arms

In a sense, he has made his arms longer. He smiles, then for the first time in a long time he stops. Elizabeth screams and pulls on the door. Simon goes white fighting with the lock.

Lynol is ever so serious, looks around and down at himself. Then the already cold room seems to get even colder. Lynol watches them all, and then Lynol's arms begin to heal at a rapid rate. In shock, Holden looks back at Simon.

"Come on, grab him! We need to strap him down!" Simon a little hesitant, but manages to go numb and blank. He runs in and grabs Lynol.

Holden jumps in and they muscle him to the bed. His gouged-out eyes are staring off to the ceiling. He continues to heal. He rambles on, "I come from a place where the laws do not apply. The laws of this perfect candidate do not apply! I will now tear down the laws of this body. My body!"

Bruce arches his back and the vibe and energy coming from him is powerful. Holden feels a force come over Bruce, but refuses to let go of him. Pearl white, Simon keeps repeating, "He's possessed. He's possessed."

They get him down on the bed. They know the procedure to patients, so instantly Lynol is strapped down. Elizabeth still tugs on the door in a now, weakened panic. Bruce heals quickly, but his arms remain unnaturally long.

Bruce smiles wide and bangs his head back on the bed while his body is completely strapped down. Then he calms and once again silence, but not for long. He fills the room with a creepy laugh. The laugh is followed with, "Eht niap si gnihton ot na latromi siht si enim!"

Holden goes to the door and begins to help Elizabeth. He pulls with all his might. Elizabeth stops and let go of the door handle, looks to Lynol lied out on the bed. She gets closer and looks over his arms.

A tear comes over her eyes. He stops moving and then looks at her with a smile. He makes eye contact even though he has no eyes. "Elizabeth, I yojne gnieb yllacisyhp esolc ot uoy. eruoy htmrow si lufthgiled…ll'I dnif uoy."

Elizabeth walks back to the door and begins to bang on it with all her might. The door swings open with ease as if the force was let up. The new nurse, Thomas Sturino is on the other side. He opens the door, "There you guys are. I was lo…"

The new nurse gets cut off while still wearing an unknowing smile. He gets pushed aside by the three running from the room. Holden's pale and Thomas can see it clearly. He grabs his shoulder, "Get the medic kit down here. Help me fix Mr. Garner's arms. Go."

Thomas runs off and Holden turns to Elizabeth, "We need to give him the adenosine serum." They look back to the dark room that they left Bruce strapped in.

He is clearly becoming somewhat of a monster. They stare into the room, then the lights flicker back on.

Chapter 12
May 18th, 1998 – 5:00 P.M.
(Time for the Solution)

Holden shoves open the door to the laboratory, Thomas comes in next to him. Holden rushes into the blue darkness. Thomas comes slightly in, right behind Holden, but stays back in the doorway. Holden catches his balance and then begins to search, frantically through the mess on top of his lit-up table and next to his lime-green squeeze ball.

Thomas makes his way in and stands next to Holden and watches while he searches, frantically. Thomas gazes around the room, clueless. He's never been in the lab, so a lot of pointless things already have his attention. "Wow!" Thomas looks at an old glass case up against the side wall. The case holds thirties-era surgical tools. Holden searches over the table, stops and looks at Thomas walking aimlessly around.

Holden shakes his head and goes to the next desk where he starts pulling open drawers. Dr. Holden gives Thomas orders while continuing his search. "Um, I'm looking for my side bag. Thomas? Thomas! Check those lockers in the back of the room." Thomas spins around and looks behind him at the lockers.

He immediately goes over to them. Holden watches him. "It will be in locker B12, I think. Well, maybe B11; I don't remember."

Thomas swings open B12 and it's empty. Holden pulls open another drawer. "I need the blood-clotting medicine so I can mix it with the adenosine when we give it to Bruce." The last drawer Holden pulls open is empty, Holden drops down on one knee, thinking.

Thomas swings open B11 and sure enough, right on top is Holden's bag. Thomas calls out, "Bingo." He comes running back to Dr. Holden with the bag. Dr. Holden meets him at his cluttered table.

Thomas hands over the bag and Dr. Holden throws it on the table and under the blinding light. He begins going through it. Holden looks frantically for the right serum and then luckily comes over an injector in his bag. He grabs the injector.

"Perfect, we need one of these." Holden stops and smiles at Thomas, then Holden brings his hand out of the bag with the coagulant.

Holden looks to Thomas and says, "I bet, it's fun watching me sweat and rush around like this. We need to get these two together and then injected into Mr. Garner."

Thomas, still without a clue of what is really going on, tries to be positive on his second day. He is slowly coming along with a lot of hints. He has to ask Holden, "So this will put him to sleep?"

Holden looks at him with complete confidence. "Yes."

***

Simon rushes around the corner back up into the lounge. Elizabeth is behind him trying to keep up but feels slightly light-headed and dizzy. Simon slows and waits for her to come up and around the corner. He walks back around and sees her struggling to get up the last few steps.

He grabs her hand and helps her up the final step and around the corner towards the lounge. She feels dizzy but fights her feelings. "I feel fine. I can walk, Simon."

He ignores her and walks with her over to the couch in the back of the lounge. She doesn't give it a second thought and throws herself down on the couch. Elizabeth takes a deep breath and throws her arms over her head while lying back. Simon watches her and can't help but notice how pale she is.

"You're sure you are okay?" Elizabeth moves her arm and makes eye contact with him. She shakes her head yes. Simon smiles, then walks away and swings open the door to his security office, his hideaway.

He goes in and sits down, confused and out of breath. He calms. It's obvious he likes sitting in here. It's the brightest room in the hospital, even with the sun setting.

He forgets it's actually daylight outside, being down in that darkness. Elizabeth lies on the couch in the hospital break room, still trying to catch her breath. She's in some sort of trance and still has the appearance of shock spread across her face. Simon sits in the security office, trying to reset himself while the sun hits his face.

He stands up and calls out to Elizabeth, "Elizabeth?" Simon waits, but no response. He understands she doesn't want to talk right now. Simon leans forward and flips on the monitors.

Elizabeth is pale and nauseous. It's not natural, rings in her thoughts, or so she thinks. Then once again out loud, "It's not natural."

Simon repeats the phrase louder and louder. Elizabeth seems to have it echo in her head, then a flash of Bruce invades her thoughts strapped to the bed. She can't handle it. They are vivid thoughts of him.

It's like a daydream. Simon gets louder still. "It's not natural." Elizabeth keeps moving forward, attempting to get off the couch.

It's slow-motion and foggy. Elizabeth sits up and tries to stand, but it's as if gravity is keeping her down, and she has to stay seated. Simon's voice keeps echoing louder in the background.

***

Holden and Thomas stand in the laboratory with the syringe and the serum for Bruce sitting on the table in front of them. Holden grabs the syringe off the table and shows it to Thomas. "Now we need to prep Bruce. We'll get Simon to give us a hand."

Holden looks at the syringe and puts it back on the table next to the scrum mixtures. Holden and Thomas leave and walk up the stairs towards the lounge. Dr. Holden looks up to the top of the stairs; he knows Elizabeth will be happy when she sees the cure for Bruce. They get to the top of the staircase and 'round the corner.

Dr. Holden instantly sees Elizabeth sitting on the couch with her head in her hands. She sits there and then looks up and makes eye contact with Holden. Their connection is broken when they hear Simon shout out loud, "It's not natural!" Holden rushes into Simon's security office, and he instantly has to cover his eyes from the light.

Holden comes in and sees Simon sitting in his chair with his back arched away from the different monitors that he's watching. It's what's on monitor four that has his eyes packed with panic, but he keeps them glued to the screen. Thomas comes into the room and turns white. He manages to whimper out, "Is that one of the patients?"

Holden says in a very serious tone, "I need to give him the serum." Elizabeth hears them talking as they converse in a loud, aggressive manner.

She gets up and asks, "What's going on?" She tries to keep her balance, but the smell of Bruce's room hits her again as if the smell of the room still lingers on her.

The reminiscence, the situation, and the experience she just went through is still with her, fresh in her thoughts. She goes to walk to the security office where everyone is, but she stops in mid-stride and then falls back down on the couch. She feels like she wants to blackout; she can't even keep her head up. Holden grips his fist tighter.

He has to rush down to Bruce. He can't take it and walks out of the security room. On the guard's screen, they watch Bruce on the camera, while he shakes violently and unnaturally, despite being tied to the bed. Simon gets closer to the screen, and then Lynol automatically stops his movement and goes still. He freezes everything except his head as he turns to face the camera.

Then he twists his head back in slow motion and looks away from the camera, and then back again. Simon and Thomas get chills up their spines. All the screens go black. Simon jumps up, caught off guard.

He looks at the black screens and then reaches over and flips the switch. Nothing. He does it again, this time toggling it. He looks at Thomas and shakes his head

"It's dead." Thomas turns around, shaken, and walks out of the security office to the lounge. Holden looks over to Elizabeth. It's clear she's sick.

He kneels down next to her. "Are you okay?"

She shakes it off and sits up. "Yeah. Yeah, I'm okay…nauseous."

Thomas comes into the lounge and sees Holden kneeling down, talking to Elizabeth. Simon follows Thomas out into the lounge and looks to Elizabeth and Holden. "The screens died." Holden stands up, confused, then they all freeze in terror instantly.

Elizabeth sits up in cold horror that shakes her reality back into her head. They all get thrown off by the creepy laughter of Bruce.

Elizabeth gets up and stands, white as a ghost. She looks over to Dr. Holden, who is standing stern and calm.

Elizabeth is not sure how to feel about him being so calm. Holden takes a deep breath. "Is that laughter?" Elizabeth nods her head in agreement. Simon loses his cool.

"Oh, man. Come on!" He paces back and forth, then rushes into his security office. He grabs a few things. He's still terrified and comes back out to help them.

Holden clenches a little then looks over to Thomas and back to Simon. "Alright, let's go take care of this. Simon, you guys, come on."

Elizabeth cringing in horror, sits back down, shaking her head no in disbelief. She watches Holden move toward the hallway that leads to the stairs. The laughter gets louder, along with a very distinct smell. Simon, cowering behind everyone, says, "Man I don't know." Holden looks back, stopping all of them

"Damn it, Simon! The medicine is down there. All we have to do is give him the damn shot."

"You hope!"

Simon takes a breath and says to the newbie nurse, "Come on, Thomas, let's go." They walk out and around the corner.

Holden looks back at Elizabeth. "We may need your help down there."

The two guys get behind Holden and begin to make their way towards the staircase. Elizabeth sits in fear while she watches the three of them go around the corner and then – silence. The three of them make their way around the corner of the lounge, facing the dark staircase that leads down. The lights below shine in the cold concrete hall and on the cold concrete floor.

Then a *crackle* and *pop* stops the laughter. It is the result of the lights turning off in the hall. Once the lights go out there is only darkness only black. But thank goodness for the silence.

Once the lights clicked off, it was all of their instincts to run back for the lounge, but for some reason, all three stick it out and hold their ground. Simon isn't stupid and at this moment appears to be the only one thinking. Simon reaches behind him and pulls out two flashlights he grabbed from his security office before coming down. Simon clicks both lights on and then hands one off to Holden.

Holden takes a breath, nervously. He has never seen anything like this before. The newbie is terrified as well, and it's clear none of them have been around anything like this in their lives. Now in the darkness, only fear shows itself when they go to take their first steps and they are unable to move.

Holden steps back and lets Simon take the lead, as he is nominated for the first one down. Simon takes a breath and leads, with Holden and Thomas on his sides. They are barely moving, scared to go forward. There is a force in this darkness and they can all three feel it.

****

Elizabeth sits on the couch and catches her breath. She listens nothing. Not sure what to do, she nervously rubs her hands through her sweaty hair. She throws her hair back behind her and ties it up.

She takes a deep breath and throws her head back, building up the courage to get off the couch and actually walk down there with them. She sits in fear. She listens, silence.

The steps are coming to an end, and it's pitch black. The fear is high and it covers all three of them while they're taking their final steps down. Holden is breathing hard and looks over to what he can see of Simon. "At least we know he is in the restraints."

Holden attempts to give any form of reassurance. The darkness is thick as they take their first steps on the hall's runway and off the stairs. The light from their flashlights seems to have a hard time defeating the darkness. They squint and can only see partway down the hall.

They all three have their feet on the pavement, walking further, toward the door at the end of the hall that holds Lynol. The light bounces off the sides at the wall as they walk through the silence. Holden looks to the side doors the further they walk. He feels uncomfortable over the silence.

It's almost unnatural like the world has been muted. They notice their light straight in front of them is shining brightly. Holden begins to shake violently at what he sees.

Holden has his vision locked forward; he's shaken and the reason why is clear. He sees Bruce. He is out of his restraints! The heavy door lies open behind his now enormous and unnatural body.

His silhouette and what evidence the light gives off suggested deformed figure. His deformed body is controlled by something not human: a monster that stands facing Simon, Thomas, and Dr. Holden. They are all three in shock at what lays before them and what they can actually see and perceive. Bruce has healed fast and has altered his physical appearance.

They notice the restraints ripped to shreds, still in his grasp. Holden looks over at Simon and sees him pierced with fear. He shakes and can hardly control the flashlight in his grasp.

***

Elizabeth gets off the couch and shakes off the stress and fear.

She has to go down there. It's clear, they may need help. It's been quiet for a minute now. Now she only needs to find the courage.

Elizabeth looks to the corner that leads down to the bottom half of the hospital, and the lights flicker on and off. The lights quickly get all their attention, but it will take more than that for them to take their eyes off of Bruce. The lights flicker on and bring on a new type of fear. The mangled-up monster's body is jaw-dropping but weirdly operational and in complete control.

Bruce wears a white straightjacket. It's torn apart with the sleeves hanging down on him. Bruce's right sleeve stretches down past his knees, with his hand sticking out of the bottom. He brings his hand up to his face and moves his fingers.

Holden inches forward to this beast that is standing before them. Lynol is motionless, while Holden inches forward toward him. "Lynol, now come on. Let's get you into the bedroom."

Holden has his hand on his holster. It's clear, he is terrified of what is in front of him. Holden thinking numerous times about even placing his hand on the holster, but this beast that stands towering in this hospital hallway is something unheard of. This beast isn't the man Bruce Garner anymore; it's the monster called Lynol. Holden and Simon stand strong, but Thomas wants dearly to fall back and runoff.

He manages to shake off the fear. The lights continue to flicker. Simon stands strong and takes a breath, trying to hold his flashlight steady on Bruce. He holds onto the flashlight while inching toward him.

Holden fights his will to stop and standstill. He forces himself to move, and they get closer. The lights flicker on and off, and Holden can clearly see Lynol's face shaking. He is twitching.

It drops Holden's stomach. "Lynol, we need you back in your room." Simon looks around and gets an instant headache from the smell of rotten eggs. Lynol stops shaking and stares straight at Holden with his head tilted.

Then their flashlights begin to flicker on and off, along with the flicker of the ceiling lights. Lynol just stares as they get a little closer. The flickers continue – then black! A bright flash blinds them, but Holden can see Lynol rush in and grab Thomas!

Lynol grabs him, all the while Lynol never taking his eyes off Holden. The lights overhead flicker back on and off. Simon only sees part of the incident. Lynol violently pulls Thomas a few feet back toward his room and then rips out Thomas's jugular.

Lynol tosses his body aside; Thomas is a bloody mess kicking on the ground. Things escalate very quickly. Simon is still in awe, and Holden is frozen and speechless. Simon drops the flashlight and rushes for Bruce.

Simon reaches Bruce and manages to get a grip on Bruce's straightjacket. Simon shoves Lynol, and he stumbles back toward his room. Simon looks back at Dr. Holden. Holden shakes it off, and then together they yell and rush Bruce.

They grab him by each arm and run him back towards his room. They get him through the doorway and back into his stained, smelly room. They end their procedure with an exhausting *umfff*, throwing Bruce into the back of the padded room. Bruce falls, hitting the back wall, and then hits the side of the bed, falling to the ground.

The lights flicker on and Simon looks to Holden, but Holden is fixed on Bruce. Bruce doesn't move; he appears unconscious. Simon, still in a rage, intends on finishing the job and goes in and attempts to put Bruce in the bed. The light goes out, but they can still see for the most part.

Simon leans in, but Holden stops him. Simon looks back at Holden then down at Bruce. "He's out."

Holden shakes his head, "No. He can't sleep. It's not that easy."

Holden has his hand on the butt of his weapon as he backs up. Bruce lies still, while the lights flicker on. They see his smile fall like a sunset – gone. It's quiet; Holden is not sure what to make of it. Maybe it is that easy.

Then there's a twitch…then another. Lynol gets unbelievable rage and leaps up with a yell. He picks up Simon with ease. The lights go out while Holden draws his gun.

He quickly backs up and points it at Lynol. Then Holden pulls the trigger, but misses! He clips the side of Lynol's torso. Simon is freaking out in Lynol's grasp.

"Son of a bitc…" Lynol heaves Simon to the back of the room against the wall. Holden takes another shot, but he doesn't have a clear view and misses. Simon screams once more in the back of the room. Then he moans in pain.

Holden gets in front of Lynol, stopping him from exiting the room. Holden yells at him, "Stop! Bruce, don't make me kill you."

Bruce stops and tilts his head, looking at Holden and the barrel of the gun staring at him. Lynol's mouth drops open and a wave of pure aggression hits Holden, launching him out the door. With ease, the force sends him down the hallway. Lynol never lifted a hand.

Holden lands with a thud and a skid. He is dazed and takes a deep breath while he lies on his back, winded. He looks down the hall, then to the gun still in his hand. Holden looks down the hall at Lynol standing in the doorway of the room.

Lynol backs up into the darkness, then the door slams shut! Holden can hear Simon's screams. Holden gets to his feet, unsure what even just happened. He can hear the screams of Simon as clear as day.

Holden sprints to the door and lets off a few rounds into the doorway. He gets to the door and shoves his shoulder into it. He bangs on the door in a complete panic. He can hear Simon's plea for help…then silence.

There's no give to the door, as Holden backs away, unsure of this complete silence. A growl gets his attention. It's faint at first, but then it gets louder. Holden backs up a few more steps, then *bang*!

Lynol sends Simon's lifeless body through the door. The door flies off its hinges and then smashes Holden down to the concrete floor. Holden sits up and sees Simon's body ripped apart, lying on top of him. He manages to get the door and Simon off himself.

He goes to stand and sees Lynol walking toward him out of the back room. The energy of this hideous man is unbearably unnatural. Holden gets up and looks to the lab where the serum is. He stands and turns to run to the lab, but Lynol is too quick and mentally grabs Simon's dead body and heaves it at Holden.

This time it sends the two of them through the lab's door, into the laboratory.

***

Elizabeth stops at the turn, frightened after hearing the gunshots followed by the other loud bangs. She turns around and walks back to the middle of the lounge, pacing back and forth. She's stressed out and runs her hands through her hair while continuing to pace. "Do something…"
Elizabeth looks to the security room and gets an idea. She goes in, and looks around the room for anything that will help her. Elizabeth stops and grabs a black baton that was stashed next to Simon's chair. Elizabeth grabs it, then takes a deep breath, looking it over. She leaves the room.

She goes out and still there is only silence. Elizabeth goes toward the staircase. She stops and listens. It's black and cold.

Elizabeth doesn't know how she does it, but she manages to force herself to go down the stairs. Elizabeth finally makes it down to the last step of the dark staircase. She forces herself the entire way down into the darkness and the silence. It's quiet and all that breaks the silence is what sounds like water drops hitting the floor.

Drip. Drip. Elizabeth stops and waits a minute; her eyes are taking forever to adjust to the blackness. Elizabeth stands still and blind in the silence.

179

The silence gets broken slightly. Even the slightest change makes Elizabeth's stomach drop. Then, again, she hears a splashing sound in the distance. Elizabeth stares into the darkness and shakes violently.

Her white shoes step off the bottom step onto the concrete floor. She can't make out what is in the distance, as she squeezes the baton tightly. She doesn't understand the gravity of the situation. The silence is unbearable.

She thinks about calling out to one of the guys, but stops. The silence is broken once again by the *whirl* of electrical power overhead. Elizabeth takes a deep breath, then the light flickers on. It's bright throughout the hallway, but she wishes the lights never turned on.

What she sees is a walking nightmare. Lynol must have heard her, or worse yet, smelt her. Lynol is in the middle of the hallway, and he stands facing her, glaring at her. Elizabeth, controlled by fear and adrenaline, has her eyes locked on him; she can only see this monster of a man watching her.

He has the most terrifying smile. Bloodstains cover him while he stands in a pool of blood on the floor all around him. Elizabeth goes numb. She wants to scream but can't. The eye contact has her heart about to stop, but then the lights go out.

It's just darkness and silence. Elizabeth, in a complete panic, tries to pick up her feet to get up the stairs, but, unable to see, she trips and falls on the staircase. Then, a flicker from the lights reveals this beast running toward her. Then darkness as she struggles, and in a second flat, the lights are back on.

Lynol's already in front of her! He's so close she can smell his breath. Lynol lets out a yell of horror. He smiles and then the lights go out.

A *blast* gets Elizabeth's attention, followed by a bright flash. Lynol's shoulder pops, and it throws his body back as blood sprays everywhere. Lynol stumbles back but doesn't take his sights off Elizabeth. Lynol falls back and rolls over, leaning up against the wall and holds his shoulder tight.

He is motionless while he stares. The lights flicker on. The gunshot came from the top of the stairs. Elizabeth looks up the stairs and sees Dr. Zazio.

He stands tall over her, wielding an enormous gun. The lights flicker back on and it brings the horror in view. Bruce is kneeling up against the wall, bleeding. Dr. Zazio comes down and sees all the blood filling the hallway evidence contributed by the bright lights.

He looks down at a terrified Elizabeth. Then Dr. Zazio puts his hand down and offers it to Elizabeth to help her up. But his hand is taken faster than it's given, as Lynol comes flying straight at Dr. Zazio. Dr. Zazio drops the gun and takes the hit at full force.

The two of them fly up the staircase. The lights go black and all Elizabeth can hear is a crash from the two of them. Elizabeth looks around in shock. Then the lights begin to flicker on and off again.

A *bang* comes from down the hallway. Elizabeth sees Holden come out of the laboratory with blood running down his face. He loses the white doctor jacket, throwing it down on the floor. He holds his syringe in his hand filled with the serum.

Elizabeth is still stunned at how fast this all happened, but she is happy to see Holden okay. Elizabeth notices Holden is standing dazed; he is the angriest she has ever seen him. He looks at Elizabeth; she's frightened but manages to get to her feet. She is still in shock, looking back toward the top of the steps.

The syringe is tight in Holden's hand as he walks toward her, looking to the top of the stairs. He is nervous, then takes a deep breath, followed with a force of pure courage to run after Bruce. He feels there is no other choice, no other way out. Dr. Holden, with his pure bravery, makes it halfway up the stairs.

He stops and is quickly thrown off by a howl followed by a scream. Elizabeth is in turmoil and frightened. She stumbles back into the hallway while looking up the stairs. She looks up to Holden and then to her right.

With another flicker of light, she sees Dr. Zazio's gun lying carelessly on the steps. Elizabeth reaches down and grabs the gun. Holden gets another burst of courage, yells aloud, and runs up the stairs toward Lynol. Elizabeth stumbles back down the hallway towards the lab and watches Holden disappear up the dark stairs and then silence.

Elizabeth takes a deep breath, looking down at the gun. She has to help, and she knows it. With the enormous gun in her hand, her heart beats fast while she looks to the stairs. She tries to get the courage, but before she can even take one step, she hears loud screams coming from Miss Walleton and Serana.

The terror that filled their screams drops Elizabeth's jaw. She has to go, but once again she's stopped and distracted. She's distracted by Holden as he comes flying back down the stairs. He hits the floor, and the syringe slides out of his grasp and up against the sidewall.

Elizabeth goes to help Holden, but the lights stop flickering altogether. Everything goes black. Elizabeth can't see anything as she stumbles back with a tight grip on the gun. A light at the bottom of the stairs flickers on in the distance.

It's the flashlight. It rolls around and beams down the hallway toward Elizabeth. Elizabeth is quiet and takes a few steps toward Holden and the flashlight. Instantly, Lynol appears!

He stands tall at the foot of the steps; the lights flicker on and off. Elizabeth's heart drops the second she sees him. In shock, she feels she can't even hold the gun up; she's paralyzed. She looks for any form of help, and then at Holden, but he's not moving.

It's clear, he's knocked unconscious, or worse, dead. She stumbles back a little farther while watching Lynol stare at her as he moves a little closer. Elizabeth looks around her, and she is already standing close to the padded room's doorway. The opening seems to be sucking her in, she can feel it behind her.

The smell of that room is stomach dropping. The hall lights stop flickering and everything goes completely black. Elizabeth backs up to the wall, next to the backroom's entrance. Lynol walks slowly towards her.

As he does, the lights behind him as he passes light up bright. Lynol is approaching with a very dark vibe. Blood covers him. He slowly walks down the hallway toward her.

He brings his arms up and points them out toward Elizabeth, then continues to walk towards her. Elizabeth feels cold come off him, all the way down the hallway. Another light gets bright behind him as he continues to walk towards her. Elizabeth has her eyes locked on him.

He almost floats off the ground as fear grips her soul. Lynol is large, aggressive, and angry while hate pours off him. He gets closer, and she can see his smile. The light comes on over

Holden's body and Elizabeth can see blood covering his head.

Lynol stops walking. With no eyes, he looks down at Holden, as the light shines down on him. Lynol mentally grabs him by the foot and heaves him back. Holden flies halfway up the stairs.

The aggression and strength that Lynol has generated from this body is terrifying. Elizabeth looks back and still refuses to go into Bruce's padded room. Elizabeth looks back to Lynol coming at her. She lets out a devastating scream, not knowing what to do.

Then she looks down to see the syringe lying up against the wall. It lies right above a bloodstain, right where Holden was lying. But Lynol has all of Elizabeth's attention, and she can't look away from this monster while he inches closer to her. She aims the gun with her last will and effort, but she can't shoot.

She sees the real him – Bruce. He walks to her with pure darkness invading him. Lynol watches her and looks her over and stops walking. She feels the wall to the room behind her.

She can't walk back any further without going into that bloody room. Elizabeth looks back behind her to the darkness. She looks through the open doorway and she can hear laughing.

"Shoot!" Lynol yells with a roar in his voice. "Shoot!" He yells again as he gets closer to her.

Elizabeth won't back into the room, but she won't kill Bruce either. She breathes deep and goes to shoot. "I'm sorry Bruce…" *Boom*

The syringe gets jabbed in Bruce's leg! Kyrose forces down on the plunger and then lets the syringe go. He watches the serum flood Bruce's flesh and you can see the serum kick in instantly. Lynol still smiles at Elizabeth.

Then like a kick of energy, his body arches back and all the lights shoot on. They shine bright and flash while Lynol convulses and roars out loud so loud it's heard in the field outside. Elizabeth sees Kyrose lying on the floor. He is terrified looking up at Lynol.

Kyrose slides back in his room, and then all the doors in the hospital slam shut and locked. Elizabeth is still terrified watching Lynol. Blood begins to pour from every wound on his body. Bruce crashes down to the ground, and then everything goes black.

Bruce is on the ground face down. Elizabeth looks to the darkness surrounding her, and then the lights kick back on with a *whirl* of power. Elizabeth looks down at Bruce, and she slowly gets the courage to move around him, but she keeps the gun on him. She walks up to Kyrose's door and twists the knob, but it doesn't turn and the door has no give whatsoever.

It's sealed shut. She still keeps her sight on Bruce while she continues to back down the hall. He lies there, and he's not moving, Elizabeth is watching him closely, waiting for him to jump up. Then a hand grabs Elizabeth's shoulder.

It's Holden. He takes a deep breath then looks over Bruce. Elizabeth looks at him and sees his face covered in blood. He's fine; it's only contributed to a small cut on his head.

Elizabeth is more than pleased to see him, but she continues to watch the unconscious Lynol. Holden looks at Elizabeth. "Keep that gun on him." Holden moves in and grabs the syringe that is still hanging out of Bruce's flesh.

Holden leans down slowly and then grabs Bruce's body. With all his might, he manages to flip him over. Bruce's bloody hand shoots up toward Holden's throat! The serum is clearly working after his arm falls short and back down to the ground, by his side.

Holden looks back at a shaken and jumpy Elizabeth. He gets to his feet and looks at Bruce's unconscious body. He gets slightly closer to get a look at the beast. He drops the empty syringe on the ground.

"Bruce is asleep." He lies still, with his head and neck limp. Bruce's smile slowly goes down, and the vibe gets lifted from the room. Holden looks around in the hall

"Whatever was here is gone."

The lights flicker a little, but nothing else. Nothing but a massacre is to be seen. Holden looks at Elizabeth, still death-gripping the gun with her finger on the trigger. Holden calmly smiles, stands up, and reaches for the gun.

"We did it, he's asleep." Holden gives another smile and a *bang* gets both of their attention. Elizabeth points the gun in the direction of the sound. She aims high toward the stairs.

She is quick to lower her weapon when she sees it's a blood-covered Dr. Zazio. He stumbles down the steps holding his arm.

Holden lets out a sigh of relief. Elizabeth, panting for air, slowly puts the gun down, but she doesn't let go just yet. She looks down at the monster lying on the floor, as he pours blood.

Bruce's body is still alive, and he's finally asleep. Serana comes out from around the corner, being pushed along by Miss Walleton. Elizabeth stands back, winded and shaking. She takes a deep breath of relief and stumbles back, dropping the gun.

Elizabeth puts her hand over her mouth, trembling in fear. Holden looks back at Dr. Zazio as he falls to his ass at the foot of the stairs. Holden goes to Elizabeth. He kneels down to grab her and holds her tight.

Elizabeth looks past his arms and sees Bruce lying in a puddle of blood. Holden, trying his best, is slowly calming Elizabeth, while she cries out loud, finally letting her guard down. They are happy that the serum worked, but Bruce is still alive, and Dr. Holden knows they need to hurry and help him if he's going to survive.

***

The prosecutor paces back and forth as a red-eyed Elizabeth tries to get a few more words out. The story gets cut off by the prosecutor. "The adenosine serum was injected, is that correct? He was completely out? Asleep?"

Elizabeth reaches under her chair and grabs a tissue and wipes her eyes. "Yes. Kyrose or Mr. Linwood saved my life by giving Bruce that shot." The prosecutor tries to wrap his head around everything and speaks out loud.

"So, if he was given the serum and put to sleep, why didn't you all just leave or call for help instantly?"

"The doors wouldn't open."

"Excuse me?"

"There was some kind of force holding the doors closed."

The prosecutor looks in wonder at the crowd. "But…he was asleep? Isn't that the point of all this? Is that Bruce or Lynol as you call him; had control of everything?"

Elizabeth adjusts herself. "Yes. He had control."

"He was asleep. I thought that was the entire solution – put him to sleep, and it all goes away."

"He was asleep, but the locks on all the doors were still sealed shut."

"Hold on, hold on! Now let's go back a little here. You are saying the doors remained locked? Now how is that even possible?"

"I honestly don't know how any of this is possible. Sir, I am a certified nurse and close to becoming a doctor, and this entire experience has made me look at life in a completely different way. And I don't know how any of this is possible." The courtroom's quiet, and the prosecutor paces and walks back to his table.

"So, the doors were locked…and phones?"

"The phones weren't in use. I know, I can't explain it."

"Okay, no phones. Escape?" The prosecutor stands back, making sure he's covering all points.

Elizabeth looks up to him. "Escape?"

She just laughs to herself and shakes her head no. "Bruce was still in control. Or, Lynol was still in control."

"Lynol…Bruce? Was he wounded?"

"Yes, he was hurt bad, and we did all we could for him while he was asleep."

"All you could? How badly wounded was he? What wounds did he obtain that had to be seen to right away? Life-threatening wounds?"

Elizabeth looks down and grabs another tissue to clean her puffy eyes. Then she points out and calls out the wounds that she could remember. "Shoulder was shot. He ripped up his arms, and he ripped up his legs with scratches."

The prosecutor goes around his table grabs a pen and writes down all she is calling out. He notices she stopped and looks up at her. Elizabeth looks away.

"He had also ripped his eyes out." The crowd gets uncomfortable with her testimony. Elizabeth looks away, brokenhearted. The prosecutor calmly lies his pen down and sits up.

"What was there you could do?"

"We did all we could."

The prosecutor looks down at his paper and grabs his pen, begins to fiddle with it. "We? Who was all to be accounted for once Bruce was finally put to sleep?" Elizabeth looks at him with shrugged shoulders.

"Well, there was Dr. Holden and Dr. Zazio. Serana and Miss Walleton were a big help with Bruce's surgeries. Then me and…the patients."

"Eight of you. What happened after Bruce woke up from being asleep for so long? Actually, why did Bruce wake up?"

"In all honesty, I don't know why Bruce woke up. And what he did after? Well, that's the real reason why we're here, isn't it?"

Chapter 13
May 19ᵗʰ, 1998 – 12:05 A.M.
(Fix Him)

The dark lab gets interrupted by a small crew of people. They have Bruce on a handheld gurney. Dr. Zazio and Elizabeth are at the head of the gurney, with Miss Walleton and Serana holding the rear. They carry Bruce into the far back of the laboratory, up to a stainless-steel table that's laid out.

It's clean and spotless, with plastic drapes hung from the ceiling all around the operating table. Dr. Zazio leads the way. "Okay, just set him up on the table. You cleaned this just like I told you right?"

All three of the nurses respond simultaneously. "Yes."

Elizabeth sets her side down on the table continues her response. "Yes, we sterilized it all, and we are set up to fix the extent of Bruce's damage."

Miss Walleton and Serana put Bruce on the table and make him comfortable. Dr. Zazio rushes off to the bathroom to clean up and get to work on Bruce. Serana lets go of Bruce's legs, still shaken and scared as she looks over him with his blood still on her. She turns to leave the room and goes out to the hallway.

Elizabeth watches Serana's face drop and go pale. The emotions are hitting her while she looks over her bloody hands. Serana leaves and Elizabeth calls out to her, "Serana!" Stopping her.

Serana turns around. "Yeah?"

Elizabeth walks to her, away from the commotion. "Are you alright?"

"Yeah. I kind of have to be."

"How did you guys get here, back at the hospital?" Serana looks at Miss Walleton and looks down.

"We were doing a hospital run with Dr. Zazio, and when we got back here, there was no one at the front gate. Once we got in, we noticed all the lights were off and Dr. Zazio got the gun from the security office. That's when we heard your scream."

Elizabeth gives her a grin. "You guys saved me. You showed up at the perfect time." Serana smiles at her and gives her a hug.

"My pleasure. I'm glad I can help." Serana walks away and further into the hall and sees the bloodstains on the concrete floor. She takes a deep breath.

"Miss Walleton and I heard the shot that Dr. Zazio let off. Then Bruce was just there! I mean, he was so angry and mean. Dr. Zazio took that hit and went down. I would be dead if it wasn't for…"

"Holden. He ran up after Bruce."

Elizabeth already knows. Serana smiles and shakes her head yes. Dr. Zazio yells from inside the lab, "I'm ready. Elizabeth? We need you in here."

Elizabeth turns to go, and Serana smiles and turns to try and find a way out of the hospital. Serana turns to Kyrose's room. The door is forced closed and locked. Serana walks over and looks inside the door's window.

Kyrose looks to the window and smiles at her. She muscles the door – no budge. It's as if a force is holding it exactly where it wants it to be. Serana makes her way down the hall and does the same to the other patients' doors along the way, but once again, they don't budge.

Robert flies up against his door in a panic. His door won't budge either. Serana yells at him. "Relax Robert! We're going to get you out of there. We'll get the door open soon."

Robert bangs the door again, then looks to the corner of the room, frightened, but there's nothing there. Serana can't handle the madness, and she runs up the stairs to the lounge.

***

Dr. Holden is in the men's room with a small medical bag scattered out on the sink. He touches up and bandages his wound; he thinks he'll be okay. Serana runs in and sees Holden coming out of the bathroom with a bandage covering his forehead while he is drying the rest of his face off. Serana looks shaken.

"We can't get out of here."

"Yeah, I know. That's why I'm doing this myself."

He points to his head and lightly touches his bandage and continues. "None of the doors will open."

"Not even the patient doors, much less the doors that lead out of the hospital." She points to the front entrance.

Holden looks around, and then goes to the doors and tries his best to open them, but no budge.

"Still, you have to be kidding me. Are we sure there's no switch or lock in case of a crisis that might be doing this?"

Serana shakes her head no while she watches Holden struggle. "Dr. Zazio says there aren't."

Serana drops her shoulders in defeat, but then she remembers. "The phones?" Serana runs into the security office and grabs the phone, but nothing. She throws it down and looks to the cellphone in her pocket.

Serana lifts it up, but there's no service; it's dead. She drops it. Holden walks over and picks it up and hands it back to Serana, then replies, "Where is Bruce now?"

"They have him downstairs prepped for surgery." Holden paces back and forth in the lounge. He rubs his hands on his face. "Okay, okay." Serana looks on the table and sees the baton that Elizabeth was once wielding. She grabs it and rushes to the window with all her might. She swings on it and the baton hits softly, no matter how hard she swings it.

They can't get out. Holden takes a sigh of defeat and looks at a terrified Serana. Dr. Holden goes back into the bathroom and begins to wash his hands. He cleans himself up and then goes back out to the lounge and looks at Serana there waiting for him.

"We need to fix Bruce. Let's go down to the lab."

The lab door swings open. Dr. Holden follows Serana into the laboratory. He goes straight to the lockers in the back of the room. Serana follows his lead.

Holden gives it a quick thought. "Just get me an apron."

Serana comes up with a white apron. Holden puts it on, tying it around his waist. "Grab a face mask also, and follow me."

Holden takes a deep breath, then goes over to the plastic draped – in area. He goes up to the plastic curtain. There's a lot of panic and shouting; it's clear it's where everybody is and they are already working on Bruce. Serana opens the curtain for him.

Holden sees Dr. Zazio taping up Bruce's right arm the best he can considering Dr. Zazio is wearing an arm brace. Luckily, Dr. Zazio has Elizabeth's help holding Bruce. Miss Walleton is overlooking Bruce's left arm. Holden stands and observes. It seems they all came to a halt for a second when Holden walks in.

Serana grabs his gloves and helps him put them on. Miss Walleton looks up at Holden and shakes her head no. "We have to cut off the arm." Holden is concerned

"Yeah, what about the other arm? Were we able to save it?"

Dr. Zazio looks up, finishing the bandage. "Yes, but no telling how well he'll be able to use it."

Holden looks over Bruce and then takes a breath with curiosity. "How stable is he?"

"He's stable enough to continue. Your serum is doing its job and thanks to the coagulant, it's even slowed his bleeding. You might have just been the one to save his life," Dr. Zazio replies, giving him all the credit.

Holden looks over Bruce, still determined. "What about his leg?"

"Other than all the scratches, his legs are okay. Not too much damage there," Miss Walleton says to Holden as she continues, "The legs are okay. Except his right arm has what I believe to be a few additional fractures, but we can't tell for sure. We don't have an x-ray machine."

Dr. Zazio walks over to the left side of Bruce, looking at the bullet wound in his shoulder. Dr. Zazio replies to Miss Walleton. "We aren't even supposed to be doing surgery here. But right now, this man's life depends on this. If we could get out, it would be a different story."

Holden jumps into the conversation. "Well, we can't. Not right now. Now we need to finish this, and it's clear that his left arm has to go. So, Miss Walleton, make the mark on his arm for the precise cut that we need to make. If he stays stable, then we'll fix his shoulder right after." Elizabeth looks at Holden and tries to show any form of support and gratitude. Serana wheels a side table over to the left side of Bruce and then props up his deformed left arm on the table.

Miss Walleton comes over with a marker and makes the mark, double-checking her work and making sure the marks are in the exact right place. Holden walks out of the surgery area and out of the curtain, held open by Serana. Holden walks out and motions for her to follow. Dr. Zazio gets all the prep and gauze ready, prepping for blood.

The curtain gets pushed aside by Serana again, followed by Holden walking back in with a surgical saw in his grasp. It's an old thirties medical tool. A piece of the old collection. Holden stops and looks at the team. He motions to Serana to cover his face. She grabs the mask and runs around, tying it on for him.

Holden goes over to the nurses and Dr. Zazio. He looks at the mark, makes his own judgment, and then places the blade on the flesh of the bicep, right under the shoulder. Dr.

Holden begins to rip through his flesh with the saw. Blood sprays the plastic curtain. In a mouth-dropping moment, the severed arm flops down on the side table that Serana had wheeled over.

Elizabeth moves the table out of the way. Dr. Zazio comes in quickly and tends to his wound. Dr. Holden checks his vitals. "His heart rate is low, but I think he'll be fine."

He hands the bloody saw to Serana, and she turns and throws it down on the side table next to the limb. She is in shock; she feels like she's just dropped a murder weapon.

Holden keeps checking his heart rate and then looks over his body. "We need to do the shoulder."

Holden stands up and goes to the table of tools and looks down at the silver blades and needles. Then there is an unexpected drop of blood. Holden, confused, looks at the bright blood shine on the once clean tools. Miss Walleton looks at Holden and then down to the tools.

"Your bandage is leaking. It needs to be changed."

Miss Walleton looks up at a winded, bloody Holden and replies, "I'll do the shoulder. Dr. Zazio can walk me through it. You go get cleaned up. Elizabeth will finish Bruce's bandage with Serana's help." Miss Walleton is truly concerned for everyone. Holden looks around him at the bloody massacre and nods in agreement, walking to the plastic opening. Serana holds the curtain open for Holden and follows him out. "You okay?"

Holden takes a breath and then replies, "I will be. I need to get cleaned up. Then we need to clean Bruce's room. He has to be able to rest, and that's the only room he has right now."

Holden comes down the stairs from the lounge after cleaning the blood off of himself. He loses the white apron. He finishes wiping his hands off while stepping off the last step and into the hallway. He sees the plastic curtain that was covering Bruce's surgery table.

It now lies on the concrete floor with pieces of Simon's body on it. Holden looks away as this is the body's reaction to not knowing the answers.

Dr. Zazio comes out of the lab and leans in the doorway. Holden stops and looks over Dr. Zazio's shoulder to see Bruce lying on the table.

Holden makes eye contact with a beat-up and tired Dr. Zazio and asks simply, "How is he?"

Dr. Zazio replies, "He's a mess. I can't tell you if he's going to make it or not. Right now, he's stable though."

Dr. Zazio turns and looks at Bruce lying still on the table. Holden shakes his head incomplete understanding. Serana and Miss Walleton come out of Bruce's room down the hall, disgusted. Dr. Zazio looks away in disgust.

"We will move Bruce once his room's clean." Dr. Zazio hits

Holden in the chest with a pair of cleaning gloves.

Cleaning the room actually goes by quick, once they all start to work together. Elizabeth is tending to Bruce in the laboratory while the others finish cleaning Bruce's room. Elizabeth sits and watches Bruce finally asleep. The machines are doing their thing, loudly keeping Bruce alive.

Elizabeth sits and listens to the crew working in the distance. They joke a little. Finally, things are back to how they once were. Elizabeth's thoughts get interrupted by Serana struggling through the entrance to the laboratory.

"Sorry. We don't mean to bother you, but we need to move him in here." Elizabeth hears the word "him," then turns around and sees the body that Dr. Holden and Serana are bringing in. It's the rest of Simon's body wrapped in plastic.

Elizabeth sees the body and looks down and away instantly. Holden and Serana move him and set him on two tables that are pushed together. Holden looks at Elizabeth. "Don't look at him. Okay?"

Elizabeth shakes her head in agreement, or at least that's what it looks like. Holden and Serana drop him off, then go back to the padded room. They both seem to give Elizabeth a grieving look as they exit. Elizabeth almost forgot what she was thinking about after seeing Simon's body.

Elizabeth sits in the silence; then she thinks back to how they once were. She frowns, defeated. She knows they will never be the same. Elizabeth gets up and looks upon Simon's mangled body.

She almost breaks down over the facts of what has happened. She leans on the table holding his body. Then for some reason, the *beep* of Bruce's machine echoes repeatedly. She listens with a small goodbye and a whimper.

She leaves Simon covered, under Holden's good advice. Holden walks around the corner and sees Elizabeth breaking down over the death of Simon. The *beep* in the background seems to get louder and louder as she looks at Simon. Holden stands, watching her, then interrupts.

"Hey? We're finished and we need to move Bruce back into his room." The rest of the group comes down the hall, loudly.

Elizabeth touches the plastic sheet over Simon and dries her eyes. The *beep* out of Bruce's machine is quiet again.

They all come in and around Holden as he stands in the doorway. He's concerned about Elizabeth. It shows all over his face. They all look winded and dirty from the cleaning.

Dr. Zazio starts barking orders. "Holden? Come grab his left side, and we will put him on the gurney. Serana and Miss Walleton, you get his legs. We will move him and then carry him to the room."

They struggle slightly to get Bruce into his room. Kyrose watches while they carry him by on the gurney. Kyrose feels sorry for the guy, seeing him all bandaged up and barely alive. Elizabeth comes running down the hall to them and watches Dr. Zazio struggle.

It's clear, he's hurt as he struggles to hold Bruce right. Elizabeth runs up. "Dr. Zazio. Let me take that from you. Your arm needs to heal before you carry too much. You'll just end up hurting yourself more."

Dr. Zazio doesn't fight her, as she grabs the gurney behind him. He looks back. "Got it?" Elizabeth nods yes.

Dr. Zazio lets go and then rushes into the padded room, turning down Bruce's bed. Elizabeth and Dr. Holden make their way into the room, followed by Serana and Miss Walleton, all carrying Bruce. Elizabeth is amazed the room is actually clean somewhat pink, but clean. They lay him on the bed and then remove the gurney from the room.

Dr. Zazio leaves the room and Elizabeth watches over Bruce. Holden stands with her for a second while the others leave the room. Dr. Holden looks over to Elizabeth. "Are you going to stay with him?"

"Yeah for a bit."

"First round? I'll get you a chair."

Bruce lies still asleep, and Elizabeth finally has her chair. Not two minutes of sitting in it and Bruce wakes up! Holden had just walked away from Elizabeth and was about to help clean up the rest of the hospital. Dr. Zazio is sitting in the laboratory and Serana and Miss Walleton are in the upstairs bathroom.

They all stop at once, with chills up their spines. They all stop simultaneously because they hear Bruce screaming! Dr. Zazio sits in the lab with a bump still fresh on his head and a sling holding his right arm. Holden rushes into the laboratory and grabs a lot of serums and needles.

Dr. Zazio watches Holden overreact. "Who's screaming? Robert?" Holden stops and looks at Dr. Zazio.

"No, Bruce is awake."

"He is?" Dr. Zazio is excited, but nervous on the inside.

Holden grabs his stuff and replies to him, "This isn't good; it's too soon for him to be awake." Dr. Holden shows him the needles in his grasp.

Dr. Zazio jumps to his feet and follows Holden out of the room. Elizabeth sits on the edge, next to Bruce's side in his room.

To see him panicking in wonder is unbearable. He feels the bandages holding him together.

Bruce can't think straight; it's a new hell. Luckily, out of this new hell, he hears Elizabeth's voice. "Bruce, stop moving, you're hurt!" Elizabeth knows she got through to him, as he stops moving instantly.

He can hear her. She knows it when he calms and tries to speak. "It all hurts…help." Holden comes in with the medicine.

Holden rushes around in the panic of the moment. Elizabeth feeds off of it. "He needs pain killers!" Holden hands her the needles with the serum.

She shakes her head. "No, wait, he's here. He can hear me." Holden shakes his head no

"It's too soon. He needs to go back to sleep. We don't know if that's him." Dr. Zazio looks in the doorway from around the corner, listening. Bruce calms and tries again to speak.

"Help me, Elizabeth." Elizabeth looks away and Dr. Holden quickly sticks him in the leg with the needle. She sheds a tear as Bruce goes to sleep again.

Chapter 14
May 19th, 1998 – 8:05 A.M.
(We Need Out)

Screams seem to become normal, and that's never a good sign. Elizabeth and Holden come running from up in the lounge. They run down the steps and towards Bruce's room. His yells have their undivided attention. They rush down the hall and see Dr. Zazio come out of Bruce's room. They slow their strut, and from their distance, they can see past Dr. Zazio and see Bruce awake in his bed. He's confused, yelling out loud. They rush past Dr. Zazio to Bruce.

Holden and Elizabeth come into Bruce's room, and it's clear he's awake again. Holden walks in and watches him move and groan in a panic. Holden looks him over and watches his movement. "This isn't right; it's only been three hours. He shouldn't be awake again."

Elizabeth is in a sense of paranoia, looking at Holden, confused. Bruce stops moving, and then Elizabeth kneels to Bruce. "Bruce? Can you hear me?"

Holden watches them, then looks back to Dr. Zazio and runs out of the room to the lab. A few moments later, Dr. Holden shows up with a needle in his grasp. "We need to put him back to sleep." Holden goes to hit him with another needle, but Bruce coherently yells out loud, interrupting everyone.

"No! No, not yet. I need to be here for a minute."

Elizabeth, confused and in tears, asks, "Are you in there, Bruce?"

Bruce turns as to almost look at her. "Elizabeth? I'm not in control, I wasn't. I can be…I need to be here." Dr. Zazio looks at Holden's grasp, and with a quickness, Dr. Zazio snatches the needle from Holden.

He responds firmly, "We aren't putting him back down just yet." Holden looks at Dr. Zazio and quickly disagrees. "Don't you ever grab something from me like that? He needs to sleep. We don't know what he is still capable of!"

Bruce repeats himself. "I wasn't in control. I'm here."

Elizabeth grabs Bruce's hand. "Are you okay? How do you feel?"

Holden turns to sympathize with Bruce, and then looks at Dr. Zazio and grabs his needle back. "I'll leave him awake for a half-hour. Then, I trust you guys will do what's necessary." Holden looks at all of them, and then places the needle on the foot of the bed and walks out of the room.

Holden decides to hold off for another thirty minutes, sitting alone quietly in the laboratory. Holden stands then, getting more and more antsy. He paces back and forth, then walks up to the doorway leading out of the lab. Holden looks around the hall, then toward Bruce's room.

He walks out of the laboratory and out into the hall. He goes towards the end of the hallway, towards Bruce's room. He can hear Elizabeth and Dr. Zazio talking; it's simple chatter. Holden keeps walking and begins to make out words, as he is eavesdropping.

He hears Bruce's voice, but he can't make out what he says. Holden looks at his watch, concerned with this situation and not at all trusting it. He comes up to Bruce's door and peeks in and around the corner. He keeps listening to them talk.

He looks in and sees a list of notes in Dr. Zazio's hands. He's actually getting notes on the entire situation. Elizabeth is leaning almost out of her chair, holding Bruce's one good arm. They continue on, and they don't see Holden as he looks over the room.

He watches for a second, then back down at his watch. He turns to go back to the lab and glances in the room one last time. He stops in his tracks and swears if Bruce had eyes, he would be looking straight at him right now. Holden shakes it off and walks back to the laboratory.

He gets to the doorway, looking in at the dark blue mess. Holden goes to his table and throws himself back in his chair.

Holden puts his arms on his head, looking directly up at his watch as he lowers his arms. His watch gets unreasonably close to his face.

Holden sits and watches the hands go by. He stands up inpatient. He continues to pace. He rubs his face then looks at his rolling chair and to the doorway. He makes a move.

Holden leans back on his rolling chair that he has drug out from the laboratory into the hall. He wanted to listen in on the conversation taking place by the three of them: a doped-up Bruce, Dr. Zazio, and Elizabeth. Holden leans back and looks at his watch again Bruce has been awake now for one hour and ten minutes. The anxiety is eating at Holden.

He knows keeping him awake is a problem, or at least it could be. Bruce is now sitting upright, trying to be hospitable and aware. They put a metal restraint on his one good arm, locking him to the metal bed frame. The restraint is on, and it's clearly an emotional moment between them, as they pry at Bruce's side of the story, of what he remembers.

Bruce keeps trying to pick up his arm, and it clanks as the cuffs catch the bed frame. Bruce feels lost, and the restraint makes him even jitterier. He is confused. He can't see but tries his best to communicate

"I was in a tunnel. It felt like a dream after a certain point in time."

Elizabeth sits closer to the side of the bed. "What is the last thing you do remember?"

Bruce tries to smile a little, but his face is torn and chapped. He replies, "I was talking to you. I had told you that…I enjoy being physically close to you. I don't know. That was the last thing I remember."

Elizabeth gets a confused look across her face. She honestly doesn't remember that. Holden comes into the doorway after getting off his chair. He looks over Bruce.

"You look better." Bruce doesn't know who's talking to him.

Holden comes in and continues. "Bruce. If you feel better, how about opening the doors?"

Bruce stops and doesn't reply for a minute. Elizabeth looks at Holden then watches Bruce. "Can you let us out of here Bruce?"

Bruce clanks as he looks over to her.

"I can't; I'm still not in control." Holden gets antsy. Bruce looks over everyone and is silent. He once again tries to use the hand that's strapped down.

Clank. Then he looks at the two of them before becoming an emotional wreck. Elizabeth looks curiously at Bruce over his simple tone. "Bruce, are you tired? You think you can go to sleep on your own?"

Bruce's voice drops a little. "Well when the body sleeps, another spirit awakes in it, bound by the personality built into this body." They all look at each other, confused. Holden is quick to respond.

"We need to put him to sleep. Now." Dr. Zazio gets up and confronts Holden,

"You can leave if you like. Look, saving this man's life is to get him to sleep on his own. He needs to sleep on his own, to get him back in control of himself."

"Now is not the time for studies, while we are trapped in here." Holden looks at Bruce and Elizabeth.

He turns to Dr. Zazio. "Can I talk to you alone in the laboratory?"

Holden looks back to Elizabeth while they are exiting the room. "Do what needs to be done, Elizabeth." Holden points at the needle he has left in the room.

Holden knows Bruce has talked long enough. He marches to the laboratory's door. Dr. Zazio casually follows a pissed-off Holden. Holden goes into the laboratory, walks into the back of the room, and looks into a mirror. He rips off his bandages, flinching slightly.

Dr. Zazio comes into the lab and flinches also when he sees Holden yank his bandage off. He walks back to where

Holden is. Holden looks over his wound. "Why do you want him to stay awake?"

Dr. Zazio avoids the question, walking back toward the door. "I think you should keep the bandage on. It might get infected." Holden looks at him through the mirror.

"So, you're avoiding my question?" Holden throws down the bandage and turns around to confront Dr. Zazio.

Dr. Zazio tries to explain himself. "Look I never said that."

"You lie."

"I want him to stay awake so he can try and open the damn doors!"

Holden gets even more defensive. "He said he can't. You know if anything happens in the time, he's awake, it's on you."

Dr. Zazio blows him off slightly. "I need coffee. Can we take this conversation upstairs?" Holden just looks at him in disgust.

Holden turns around from him about to go back to dealing with his bandages, then looks over his table to his serum. Holden rubs his face and notices one of the vials of Dr. Zazio's serum is missing. The serum 2544 is nowhere to be found. Dr. Holden turns around.

Dr. Zazio is about to walk off and get a coffee. Holden chuckles. "No way. You son of a bitch."

Dr. Zazio turns back around, "I beg your pardon?"

"You son of a bitch! You woke him up!" Holden runs up to Dr. Zazio and grabs him by the jacket and heaves him back into the lab. Dr. Zazio hits and falls into a rolling chair.

Dr. Holden is on him in a flash and aggressively grabs him. "You woke him up! Why?"

Elizabeth over hears the shouting, she gets wide eyed over the comment. Then Elizabeth turns and watches Bruce's head shake and wobble around. It looks like he's having trouble holding it up. She is a little off guard. "Bruce? Bruce, do you think if you lie back down it would help you go to sleep?"

Bruce tries once again to lift his one good arm. *Clank.* He looks down at the restraint, *clank*, and replies, "Sleep? That's what you need to clean the body of any entity."

Elizabeth looks at him, confused, as he slumps over. She looks over to the needle lying on the foot of the bed.

She looks at Bruce and he just sits then, *clank*. Then he again comments, "In return, you become one of these entities filling the body. I guess it's mine now…" He slurs lightly. Elizabeth looks at the serum again, then back at Bruce. He still sits, but what she doesn't notice is that the restraint isn't clanking anymore…because it's off.

She stands and goes for the serum and bends down to get it. She turns back around, and Bruce stands in front of her and he starts to smile. Dr. Holden hits Dr. Zazio across the mouth. Dr. Zazio replies, "I want him to unlock the doors! He's our only way out." Holden looks at him in disbelief and disgust. He goes to take another swing but is caught off guard when he hears Elizabeth's blood-curdling scream! Holden, without hesitation, lets go of Dr. Zazio and runs out of the laboratory.

***

The prosecutor runs his hands through his hair, slightly sick to his stomach. Elizabeth finishes her story. It's clearly written on everyone's faces, the confusion on how she's still alive. The prosecutor stands and walks out in front of Elizabeth.

"There were two attacks?"

Elizabeth leans forward to the microphone and replies, "Yes. Two attacks on the staff at Necropolis Hospital." The prosecutor, in a shock of amazement, is acting like he hasn't heard the story before.

He looks at the judge in disbelief, then back at Elizabeth. He continues, "How did the doors open?"

Elizabeth, in a small confusion, replies, "I don't know. I assume Bruce did it. Maybe to get to the patients, which he did. Or, it was him simply walking out of the hospital. I don't know."

"Miss Primrose, will you say out loud I'm sure everyone wants to know why you don't know? Please say it so everyone that is here today knows why."

"I don't know what happened because I was knocked unconscious. Bruce left me there. I guess he felt that he hit me so hard that I had to be dead. Then after that second attack, I was woken up by people putting me on a gurney, and I was about to be airlifted out of Necropolis Hospital." Elizabeth looks away, ashamed that she survived the attack.

"But when I was leaving, and they were taking me out, I could see the break room and it was a mess with blood and body parts."

Elizabeth's eyes water up like never before. "All of them are dead." The prosecutor quickly rephrases her

"All of them are dead except one, and of course, yourself," the prosecutor announces. He shakes it off and goes back to his table. The flashing of a memory comes to

Elizabeth, and it drops her face. Wilson stands up and looks to Elizabeth.

Elizabeth then hears the prosecutor say, "It was one doctor. He and yourself seemed to survive the attack when everyone believed no one could."

Elizabeth is finally at ease on the stand, like a weight had been lifted. The prosecutor smiles at Elizabeth then turns to the judge. "I hold all questions for the time being. Miss Primrose is free to go."

The judge nods, turns to Elizabeth, and gestures for her to leave the stand. He then speaks, "Do you have another witness to call to the stand?" Elizabeth gets off the stand and walks back over toward her side of the courtroom.

Wilson smiles at Elizabeth while standing. She looks at him in a sigh of relief, as Wilson watches Elizabeth walk over. She gets to the side of the table, looking at Wilson as he begins. "I would like to call Dr. Zazio to the stand."

Elizabeth dies a little inside when she hears his name. She knows now Holden never made it out of that hell alive. Elizabeth, in a small sigh of defeat, sits down at the table. The doors in the back of the courtroom open and Dr. Zazio walks in.

You can hear instantly the crowd mumbling about. He limps in, still beat up from head to toe. He sees Elizabeth and makes complete eye contact, then looks away. Elizabeth has her eyes locked on him.

Bad vibes roll-off him…guilt. Wilson walks over to the judge's stand as Dr. Zazio is being sworn in. Wilson finishes with the judge and goes back to Elizabeth and leans in and tells her, "You can leave now. You can go home until we call you again."

He smiles at her and then walks back over to Dr. Zazio, who is taking the stand. Elizabeth makes her way to the back of the courtroom. On the way, she nods to her friends and family; some follow her to the back. Elizabeth stops and turns to see Dr. Zazio on the stand.

Wilson begins, "Dr. Zazio, what do you make of all this?"

Dr. Zazio looks at Elizabeth with her hand on the door to exit. He continues, "It's hard to tell. We basically lost a doorway to another side of this life, we may never know of, or where, he is."

***

Dr. Zazio stands stern while camera flashes go off all around him. He talks to the press after this day of the court has come to an end. He stands on the steps at the courthouse. There are a lot of cameras and questions.

One reporter is quick to ask Dr. Zazio. "Where do you think Bruce Garner is?"

"Do you think they will find him?"

Another reporter yells out loud to the doctor. Another flash, and Dr. Zazio speaks up, "I don't know where Bruce went. He is not in his right state of mind to survive. He could actually be anywhere."

"Do you think you will ever see him again?" Dr. Zazio's expression changes and he replies, "That's all for me today. Thank you, guys, so much." Dr. Zazio turns to walk away and the press goes crazy shouting questions at the doctor, as he turns away from them.

Dr. Zazio walks away back into the courthouse. Elizabeth stands with Tamara and Jordan in the distance. She walks away after watching Dr. Zazio talk on the steps. Dr. Zazio makes his way through to the parking garage.

He takes his time getting down there; with his hurt leg and shoulder. He gets into the garage, then makes another turn going toward his car. It's quiet, then he's cut off by Elizabeth. She casually walks up to him.

"So, do you think you're going to see him again?"

"Hello, Elizabeth." Elizabeth walks up closer to him.

"How did you get out of there? How are you still alive?"

"You ask me that like you're disappointed."

Elizabeth walks past him, "I'm not, I now remember you standing tall outside your hospital when they carried me out. I'm just confused about what your intentions were on this whole thing."

"I hid."

"You hid?"

Elizabeth about to walk away, stops to make another reply, "You know, all that serum ended up missing. All of it." Elizabeth walks toward the elevator and pushes the button.

Dr. Zazio watches her with a scowl coming across his face, "I was only trying to help Mr. Garner, it feels like…are you trying to say something?" *Ding* Elizabeth walks into the elevator then the doors slide closed.

Chapter 15
May 27th, 1998 (Going Home)

At the new hospital Dr. Zazio is working at while Hospital Necropolis gets cleaned and remodeled. Dr. Zazio waves to his passing associate while leaving the hospital. The thoughts of the incident are still fresh in his mind. He still wants to take his studies further on the subject. He doesn't plan to stop. He walks out into the dark night and the cold wind. He steps out of the doors and then off the curb. He searches through his suit jacket's pocket.

Then a beep and his car unlocks in the distance. He shrugs his shoulders over the cold breeze. He picks up pace as another rough breeze blows by. He rushes over and yanks on the door handle and swings the door open.

He jumps in his car. He's eager to start it up and leave. He shoves the key in the ignition and turns over the engine. The Lincoln lights up with warmth and loud music.

Dr. Zazio jumps over the loud music and hits the power button. He sits in the cold. A cold drift blows over his shoulder from the car's vents; he gets the chills. He freezes up and slowly looks in the back seat and like always nothing's there.

He throws the car in gear and turns the headlights on. The lights catch a dark figure in the distance. Dr. Zazio looks further then *bang!*

There's a knock on his window.

Dr. Zazio almost has a heart attack. It's only his friend. His associate he passed in the hall. He now stands outside Dr. Zazio's car window.

He waves his forgotten portfolios in the window. Dr. Zazio rolls down the window. "Dr. Zazio you can't forget these. They are all your new patients."

"Yes, of course."

Dr. Zazio casually looks him over, "I can't believe I forgot them. My mind is off the reservation." He grabs the portfolios and puts them on the passenger seat.

The man turns and walks off. "Have a good night, doctor." He waves again to the doctor and then continues on back into the hospital. Dr. Zazio looks over the portfolios and actually gets slightly irritated.

He wants to get home. He feels as if he hasn't been there all month. Dr. Zazio laughs a little under his breath and then shakes his head. Then backs up out of the parking lot, on his way home.

Dr. Zazio looks to his passenger seat after he merges onto the freeway to go home. The files from the hospital are the new patients that Dr. Zazio is already handling and giving treatment to. They are all neurologists' cases. He reaches over and grabs a few files and looks them over.

He hits his signal and merges into traffic, just long enough to take the next exit out onto a second freeway. His foot is down on the gas pedal. He merges and hits the cruise control. He looks at the files, then throws them back on the passenger seat.

He drives out for a few miles. He's going home. He exits and then makes a left through a small side town. He keeps going, then it's darkness.

He keeps driving out; ready to see the lights of his house sitting on his land. They will be shining on the hilltop any minute. He's ready to be home after this court date, and events altogether. The lights of his house show slightly, but nothing compared to the reflection of the stalled car that appears right in front of him on the road!

The old, dirty station wagon appears over the hill instantly, stopped! Dr. Zazio sees it for a slight second, but nothing he could do. He ends up ramming into the rear end of the stalled car. Dr. Zazio hits and for a split second, he sees the car in its entirety.

It's an old Station Wagon with no windows and not running, and from what he could see, no driver. But before Dr. Zazio hit, he could clearly see Bruce's face off to the side of the road, smiling. Dr. Zazio sees it all and then takes the hit and instantly blacks out.

***

Dr. Zazio coughs with extreme pressure on his chest. The pain wakes him up. He can't think straight from the pain. He coughs again.

He thinks he broke a rib and then goes to grab his chest. He stops not by his own choice, but to the simple fact that, he's cuffed to a chair. His arms are in complete restraint. Dr. Zazio confused, "What is this?"

He looks up and coughs again and then panic. He looks over the room; it's dark. Dr. Zazio knows this concrete floor, it's his own basement. He is in his own house.

His thought gets cut short when he hears a deep raspy voice come from behind him. "Doctor, I remember you."

Dr. Zazio fights a little as a spike of pain rises in his chest. He coughs out, "Who's that? Who is there?"

Dr. Zazio already knows the answer, but not wanting to admit it. It doesn't matter that he doesn't want to admit it, he knows. "I'm happy to have found you. It was easy after all our talks… I need help." Dr. Zazio coughs up blood, hurt.

He tries to reason, "Then come out and untie me. I'm a doctor and I promise I can help you." He hears something drop, and it clearly implies that whoever is behind him is coming closer. A right hand comes over Dr. Zazio as he sits in restraint.

The rough grasp gets into view. Dr. Zazio's breath gets less and less. He sees Bruce's chewed up fingers come over his shoulder. As Bruce gets closer, Dr. Zazio can only watch the monster come into view slowly.

He sees the chewed-up finger that leads up to a chewed-up wrist, and forearm. He's been eating himself. He walks into view breathing heavily. Dr. Zazio looks around his basement and sees piss and fesses in the corner.

Bruce has been staying down here. Dr. Zazio closes his eyes terrified. "Look Bruce or Lynol. I can help you, but you need to untie me."

Dr. Zazio jumps when Bruce responds, "Lynol? Awe, yes." Dr. Zazio looks up to Bruce standing over him. His heart stops. Bruce looks terrible, rotting away to nothing, with missing limbs and parts.

Bruce walks out and looks to Dr. Zazio with a smile spread across his face.

"I need your help."

Dr. Zazio, shaken, coughs up blood. "What? Lynol, I'll do anything."

Bruce tilts his head to him. "Who's Lynol?"

The simple words send Dr. Zazio's soul into a panic. Bruce looks at him and continues, "You see, this body is dying and I'm not finished with this adventure that I want to set out for myself."

Bruce goes over to a small shelf in the basement. He also finds a few rusty nails and tools. He finds a rusty hammer sitting in the back. Bruce picks it up with his one arm.

He turns back facing Dr. Zazio. It's not until Bruce walks back up that Dr. Zazio sees a hammer in his hand. The hammer has a sharp nail magnetized to the tip. Dr. Zazio in fear looks at Bruce.

Bruce facing Dr. Zazio looks lost holding the hammer in his hand. His head tilts, "I need to keep you awake. So, your body's defense comes down." Bruce points off to the side of the room, and what Dr. Zazio sees is jaw-dropping.

It's the 2544 serum.

"I need to keep you awake, so your defenses…fall."

"You want my body! Lynol?"

"Yes, oh so much, and I'm Spingolia."

Spingolia swings the hammer with aggression and pins the nail in the back of Dr. Zazio's head. It sticks in the exact same spot Bruce had the glass piece once imbedded. Bruce sticks the nail in his skull, and then another hard hit for good measure.

www.ingramcontent.com/pod-product-compliance
Lightning Source LLC
Chambersburg PA
CBHW071609030726
47593CB00001BA/371